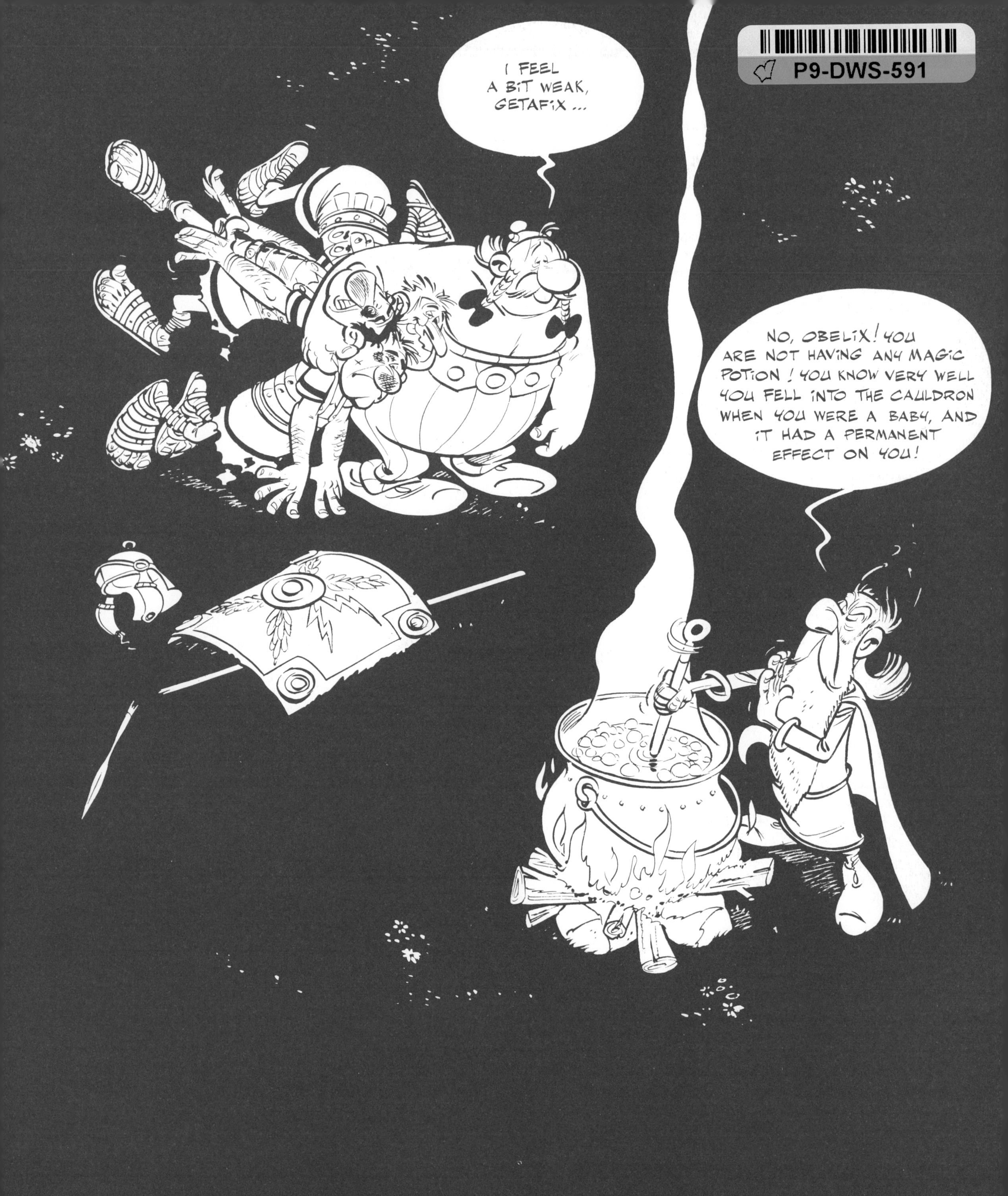
I FEEL A BIT WEAK, GETAFIX ...
NO, OBELIX! YOU ARE NOT HAVING ANY MAGIC POTION! YOU KNOW VERY WELL YOU FELL INTO THE CAULDRON WHEN YOU WERE A BABY, AND IT HAD A PERMANENT EFFECT ON YOU!

GOSCINNY AND UDERZO
PRESENT
An Asterix Adventure

ASTERIX
IN
SWITZERLAND

Written by RENÉ GOSCINNY *and Illustrated by* ALBERT UDERZO

Translated by Anthea Bell *and* Derek Hockridge

Orion
Children's Books

Asterix titles available now

1 Asterix the Gaul
2 Asterix and the Golden Sickle
3 Asterix and the Goths
4 Asterix the Gladiator
5 Asterix and the Banquet
6 Asterix and Cleopatra
7 Asterix and the Big Fight
8 Asterix in Britain
9 Asterix and the Normans
10 Asterix the Legionary
11 Asterix and the Chieftain's Shield
12 Asterix at the Olympic Games
13 Asterix and the Cauldron
14 Asterix in Spain
15 Asterix and the Roman Agent
16 Asterix in Switzerland
17 The Mansions of the Gods
18 Asterix and the Laurel Wreath
19 Asterix and the Soothsayer
20 Asterix in Corsica
21 Asterix and Caesar's Gift
22 Asterix and the Great Crossing
23 Obelix and Co.
24 Asterix in Belgium
25 Asterix and the Great Divide
26 Asterix and the Black Gold
27 Asterix and Son
28 Asterix and the Magic Carpet
29 Asterix and the Secret Weapon
30 Asterix and Obelix All at Sea
31 Asterix and the Actress
32 Asterix and the Class Act
33 Asterix and the Falling Sky
34 Asterix and Obelix's Birthday – the Golden Book
35 Asterix and the Picts
36 Asterix and the Missing Scroll

Where's Asterix?
Where's Dogmatix?
Asterix and the Vikings
Asterix at the Olympic Games (film tie-in)
How Obelix Fell into the Magic Potion
Asterix Omnibus 1 (Books 1-3)
Asterix Omnibus 2 (Books 4-6)
Asterix Omnibus 3 (Books 7-9)
Asterix Omnibus 4 (Books 10-12)
Asterix Omnibus 5 (Books 13-15)
Asterix Omnibus 6 (Books 16-18)
Asterix Omnibus 7 (Books 19-21)
Asterix Omnibus 8 (Books 22-24)
Asterix Omnibus 9 (Books 25-27)
Asterix Omnibus 10 (Books 28-30)
Asterix Omnibus 11 (Books 31-33)

ORION CHILDREN'S BOOKS

This revised edition first published in 2004 by Orion Books Ltd
This edition published in 2016 by Hodder and Stoughton

7 9 10 8 6

Original title: *Astérix chez les Helvètes*
Exclusive licensee: Hachette Children's Group
Translators: Anthea Bell and Derek Hockridge
Typography: Bryony Newhouse

A CIP record for this book is available from the British Library

ISBN 978-0-7528-6634-5 (cased)
ISBN 978-0-7528-6635-2 (paperback)
ISBN 978-1-4440-1323-8 (ebook)

Printed in China

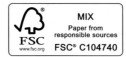

MIX
Paper from responsible sources
FSC® C104740
FSC www.fsc.org

Orion Children's Books
An imprint of Hachette Children's Group, part of Hodder and Stoughton
Carmelite House, 50 Victoria Embankment
London EC4Y 0DZ
An Hachette UK Company

www.hachette.co.uk
www.asterix.com
www.hachettechildrens.co.uk

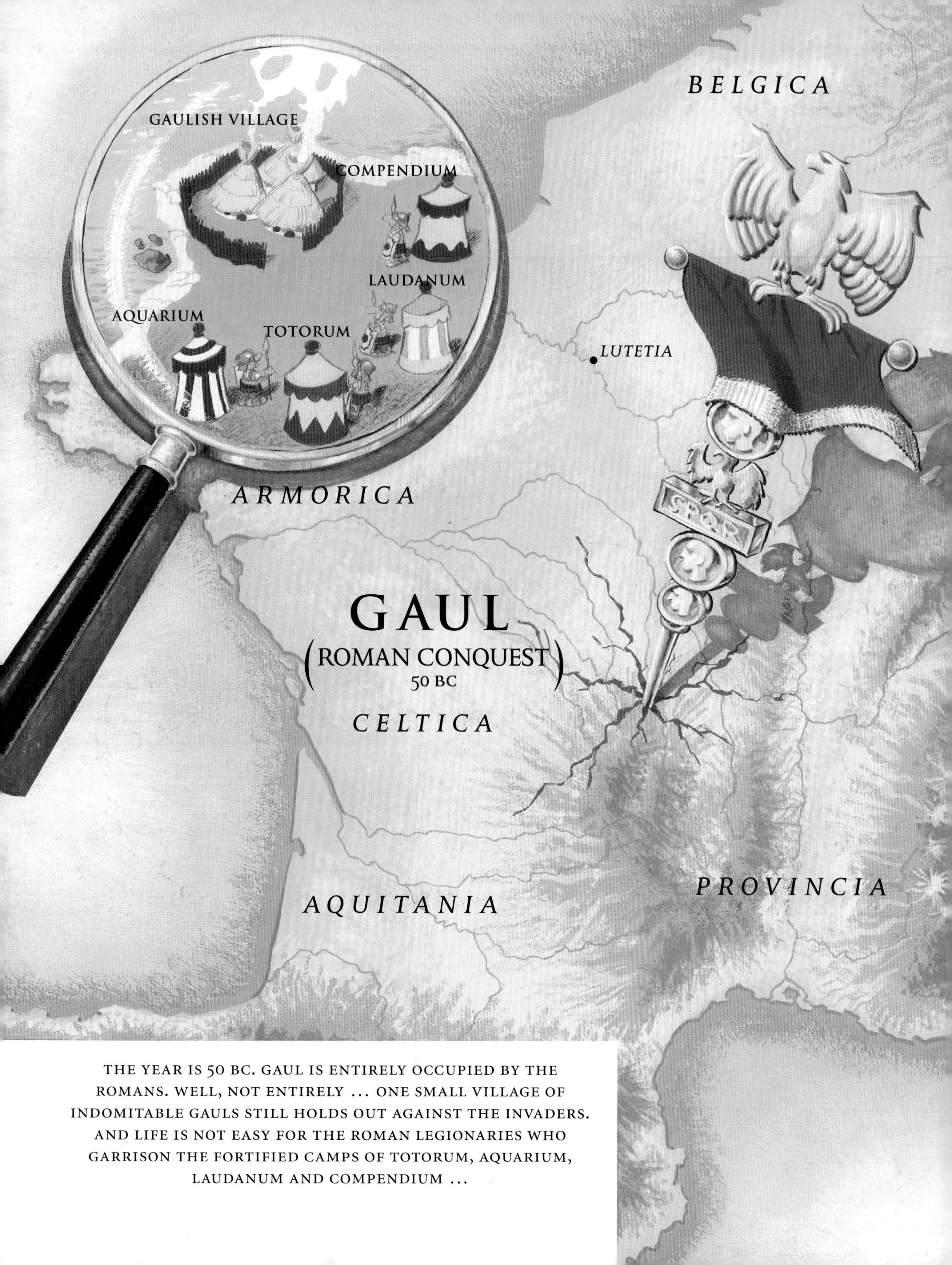
BELGICA
GAULISH VILLAGE
COMPENDIUM
LAUDANUM
AQUARIUM
TOTORUM
LUTETIA
SPQR
ARMORICA
GAUL
(ROMAN CONQUEST)
50 BC
CELTICA
AQUITANIA
PROVINCIA

THE YEAR IS 50 BC. GAUL IS ENTIRELY OCCUPIED BY THE ROMANS. WELL, NOT ENTIRELY ... ONE SMALL VILLAGE OF INDOMITABLE GAULS STILL HOLDS OUT AGAINST THE INVADERS. AND LIFE IS NOT EASY FOR THE ROMAN LEGIONARIES WHO GARRISON THE FORTIFIED CAMPS OF TOTORUM, AQUARIUM, LAUDANUM AND COMPENDIUM ...

ASTERIX, THE HERO OF THESE ADVENTURES. A SHREWD, CUNNING LITTLE WARRIOR, ALL PERILOUS MISSIONS ARE IMMEDIATELY ENTRUSTED TO HIM. ASTERIX GETS HIS SUPERHUMAN STRENGTH FROM THE MAGIC POTION BREWED BY THE DRUID GETAFIX . . .

OBELIX, ASTERIX'S INSEPARABLE FRIEND. A MENHIR DELIVERY MAN BY TRADE, ADDICTED TO WILD BOAR. OBELIX IS ALWAYS READY TO DROP EVERYTHING AND GO OFF ON A NEW ADVENTURE WITH ASTERIX − SO LONG AS THERE'S WILD BOAR TO EAT, AND PLENTY OF FIGHTING. HIS CONSTANT COMPANION IS DOGMATIX, THE ONLY KNOWN CANINE ECOLOGIST, WHO HOWLS WITH DESPAIR WHEN A TREE IS CUT DOWN.

GETAFIX, THE VENERABLE VILLAGE DRUID, GATHERS MISTLETOE AND BREWS MAGIC POTIONS. HIS SPECIALITY IS THE POTION WHICH GIVES THE DRINKER SUPERHUMAN STRENGTH. BUT GETAFIX ALSO HAS OTHER RECIPES UP HIS SLEEVE . . .

CACOFONIX, THE BARD. OPINION IS DIVIDED AS TO HIS MUSICAL GIFTS. CACOFONIX THINKS HE'S A GENIUS. EVERY-ONE ELSE THINKS HE'S UNSPEAKABLE. BUT SO LONG AS HE DOESN'T SPEAK, LET ALONE SING, EVERYBODY LIKES HIM . . .

FINALLY, VITALSTATISTIX, THE CHIEF OF THE TRIBE. MAJESTIC, BRAVE AND HOT-TEMPERED, THE OLD WARRIOR IS RESPECTED BY HIS MEN AND FEARED BY HIS ENEMIES. VITALSTATISTIX HIMSELF HAS ONLY ONE FEAR, HE IS AFRAID THE SKY MAY FALL ON HIS HEAD TOMORROW. BUT AS HE ALWAYS SAYS, TOMORROW NEVER COMES.

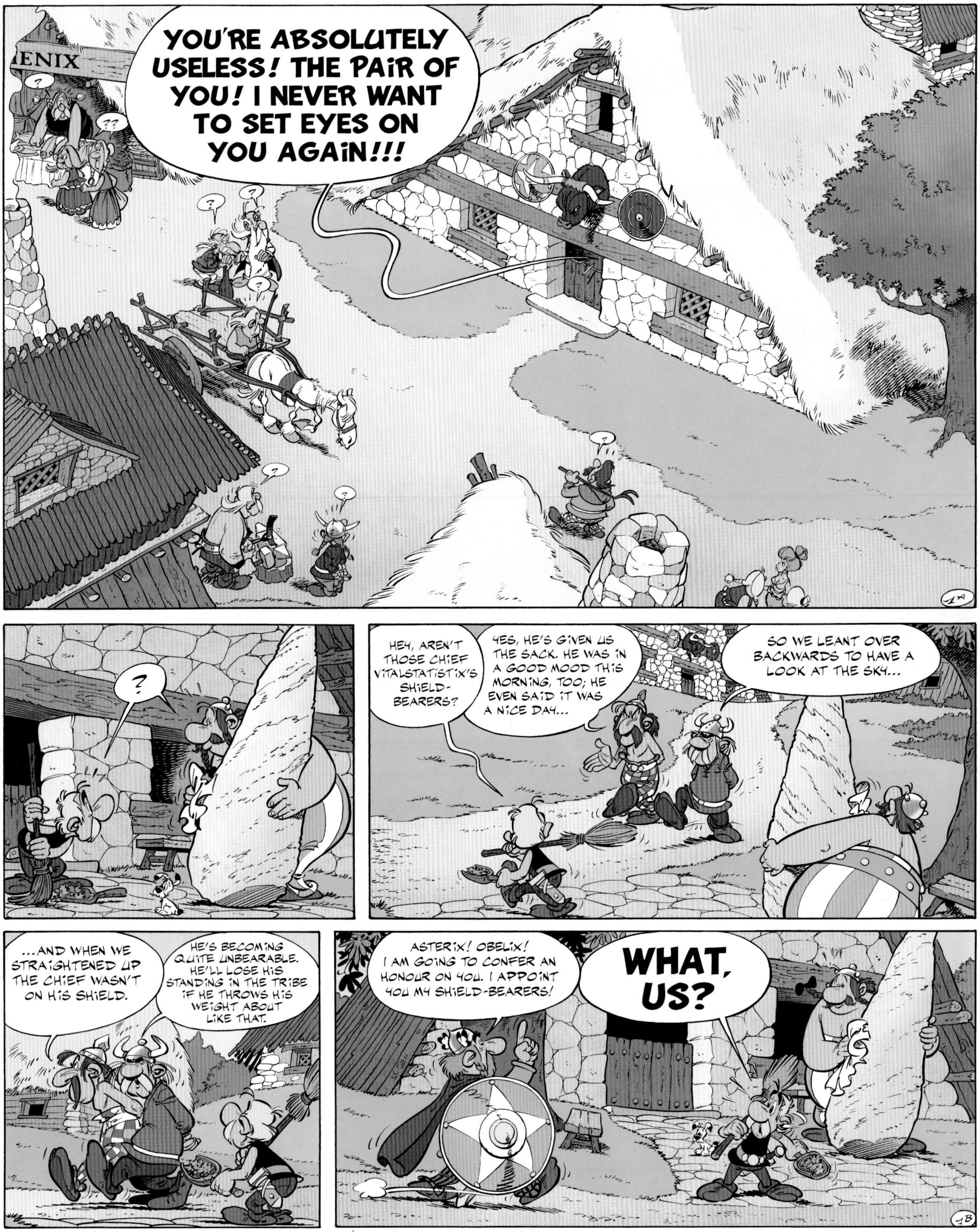

ENIX
YOU'RE ABSOLUTELY USELESS! THE PAIR OF YOU! I NEVER WANT TO SET EYES ON YOU AGAIN!!!
?
??
?
?
?
?
?
HEY, AREN'T THOSE CHIEF VITALSTATISTIX'S SHIELD-BEARERS?
YES, HE'S GIVEN US THE SACK. HE WAS IN A GOOD MOOD THIS MORNING, TOO; HE EVEN SAID IT WAS A NICE DAY...
SO WE LEANT OVER BACKWARDS TO HAVE A LOOK AT THE SKY...
...AND WHEN WE STRAIGHTENED UP THE CHIEF WASN'T ON HIS SHIELD.
HE'S BECOMING QUITE UNBEARABLE. HE'LL LOSE HIS STANDING IN THE TRIBE IF HE THROWS HIS WEIGHT ABOUT LIKE THAT.
ASTERIX! OBELIX! I AM GOING TO CONFER AN HONOUR ON YOU. I APPOINT YOU MY SHIELD-BEARERS!
WHAT, US?

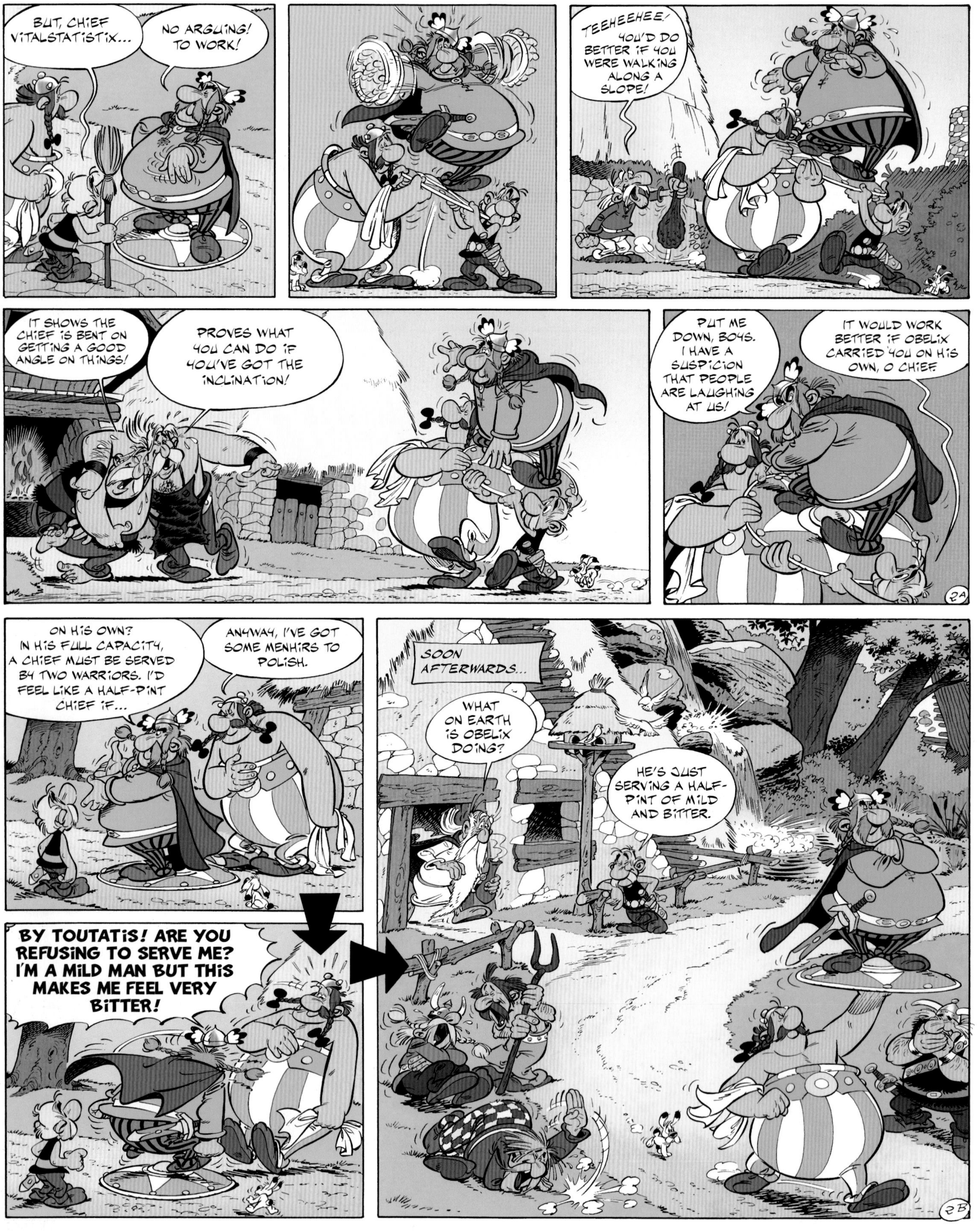
BUT, CHIEF VITALSTATISTIX...
NO ARGUING! TO WORK!
TEEHEEHEE!
YOU'D DO BETTER IF YOU WERE WALKING ALONG A SLOPE!
POC! POC! POC!
IT SHOWS THE CHIEF IS BENT ON GETTING A GOOD ANGLE ON THINGS!
PROVES WHAT YOU CAN DO IF YOU'VE GOT THE INCLINATION!
PUT ME DOWN, BOYS. I HAVE A SUSPICION THAT PEOPLE ARE LAUGHING AT US!
IT WOULD WORK BETTER IF OBELIX CARRIED YOU ON HIS OWN, O CHIEF.
2A
ON HIS OWN? IN HIS FULL CAPACITY, A CHIEF MUST BE SERVED BY TWO WARRIORS. I'D FEEL LIKE A HALF-PINT CHIEF IF...
ANYWAY, I'VE GOT SOME MENHIRS TO POLISH.
BY TOUTATIS! ARE YOU REFUSING TO SERVE ME? I'M A MILD MAN BUT THIS MAKES ME FEEL VERY BITTER!
SOON AFTERWARDS...
WHAT ON EARTH IS OBELIX DOING?
HE'S JUST SERVING A HALF-PINT OF MILD AND BITTER.
2B

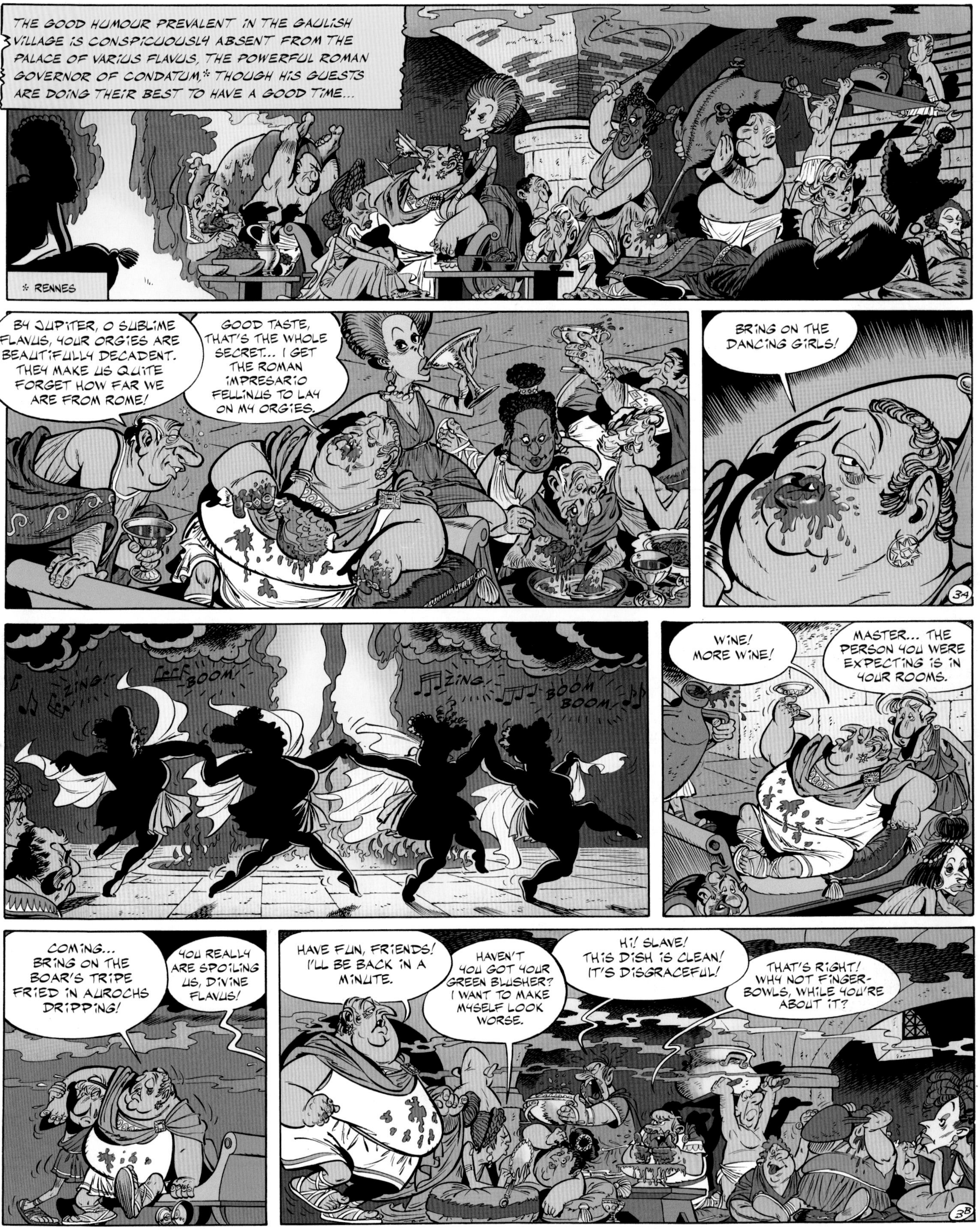

THE GOOD HUMOUR PREVALENT IN THE GAULISH VILLAGE IS CONSPICUOUSLY ABSENT FROM THE PALACE OF VARIUS FLAVUS, THE POWERFUL ROMAN GOVERNOR OF CONDATUM,* THOUGH HIS GUESTS ARE DOING THEIR BEST TO HAVE A GOOD TIME...
* RENNES
BY JUPITER, O SUBLIME FLAVUS, YOUR ORGIES ARE BEAUTIFULLY DECADENT. THEY MAKE US QUITE FORGET HOW FAR WE ARE FROM ROME!
GOOD TASTE, THAT'S THE WHOLE SECRET... I GET THE ROMAN IMPRESARIO FELLINUS TO LAY ON MY ORGIES.
BRING ON THE DANCING GIRLS!
ZING!
BOOM!
ZING!
BOOM BOOM!
WINE! MORE WINE!
MASTER... THE PERSON YOU WERE EXPECTING IS IN YOUR ROOMS.
COMING... BRING ON THE BOAR'S TRIPE FRIED IN AUROCHS DRIPPING!
YOU REALLY ARE SPOILING US, DIVINE FLAVUS!
HAVE FUN, FRIENDS! I'LL BE BACK IN A MINUTE.
HAVEN'T YOU GOT YOUR GREEN BLUSHER? I WANT TO MAKE MYSELF LOOK WORSE.
HI! SLAVE! THIS DISH IS CLEAN! IT'S DISGRACEFUL!
THAT'S RIGHT! WHY NOT FINGER-BOWLS, WHILE YOU'RE ABOUT IT?

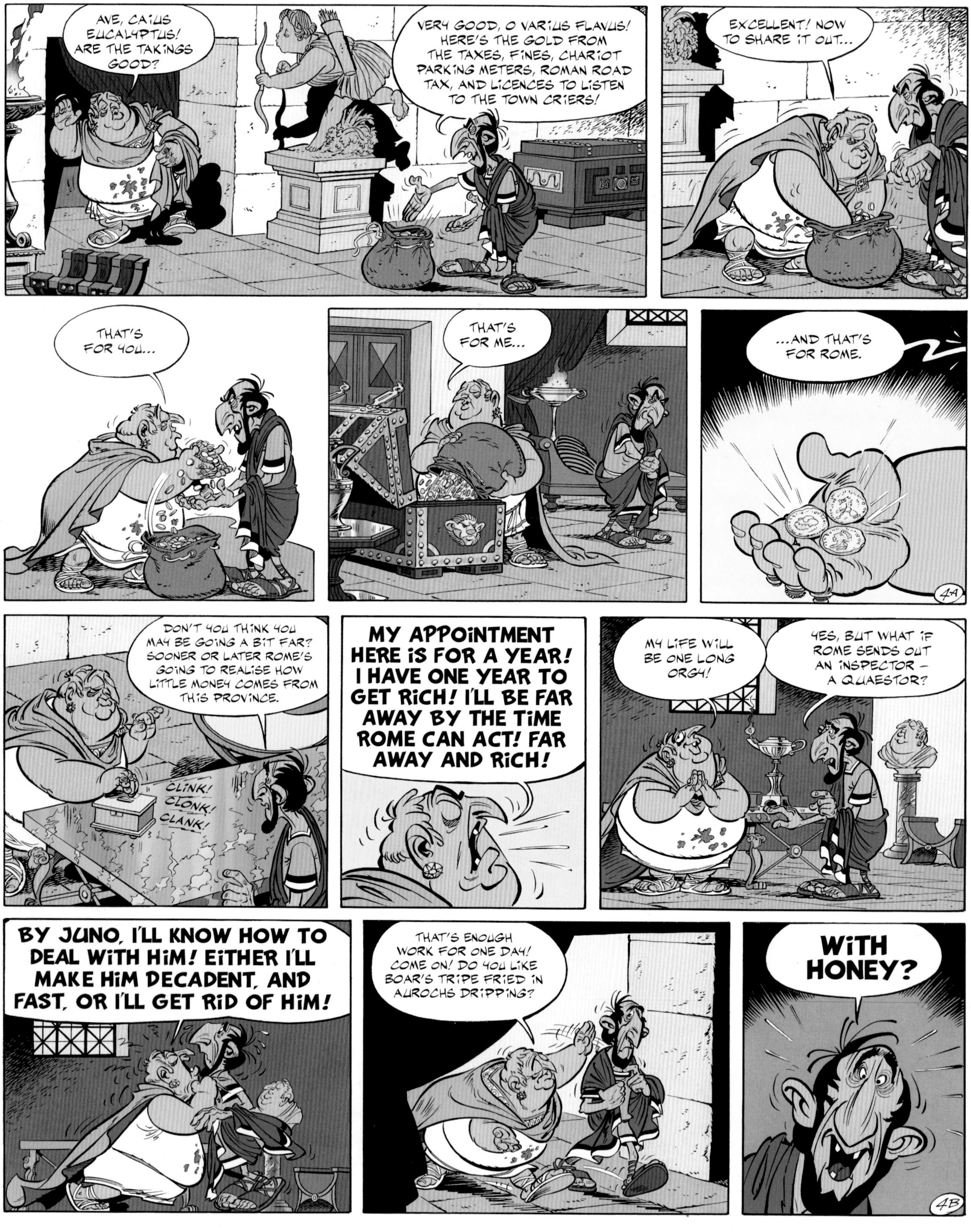
AVE, CAIUS EUCALYPTUS! ARE THE TAKINGS GOOD?
VERY GOOD, O VARIUS FLAVUS! HERE'S THE GOLD FROM THE TAXES, FINES, CHARIOT PARKING METERS, ROMAN ROAD TAX, AND LICENCES TO LISTEN TO THE TOWN CRIERS!
EXCELLENT! NOW TO SHARE IT OUT...
THAT'S FOR YOU...
THAT'S FOR ME...
...AND THAT'S FOR ROME.
4A
DON'T YOU THINK YOU MAY BE GOING A BIT FAR? SOONER OR LATER ROME'S GOING TO REALISE HOW LITTLE MONEY COMES FROM THIS PROVINCE.
CLINK! CLONK! CLANK!
MY APPOINTMENT HERE IS FOR A YEAR! I HAVE ONE YEAR TO GET RICH! I'LL BE FAR AWAY BY THE TIME ROME CAN ACT! FAR AWAY AND RICH!
MY LIFE WILL BE ONE LONG ORGY!
YES, BUT WHAT IF ROME SENDS OUT AN INSPECTOR – A QUAESTOR?
BY JUNO, I'LL KNOW HOW TO DEAL WITH HIM! EITHER I'LL MAKE HIM DECADENT, AND FAST, OR I'LL GET RID OF HIM!
THAT'S ENOUGH WORK FOR ONE DAY! COME ON! DO YOU LIKE BOAR'S TRIPE FRIED IN AUROCHS DRIPPING?
WITH HONEY?
4B

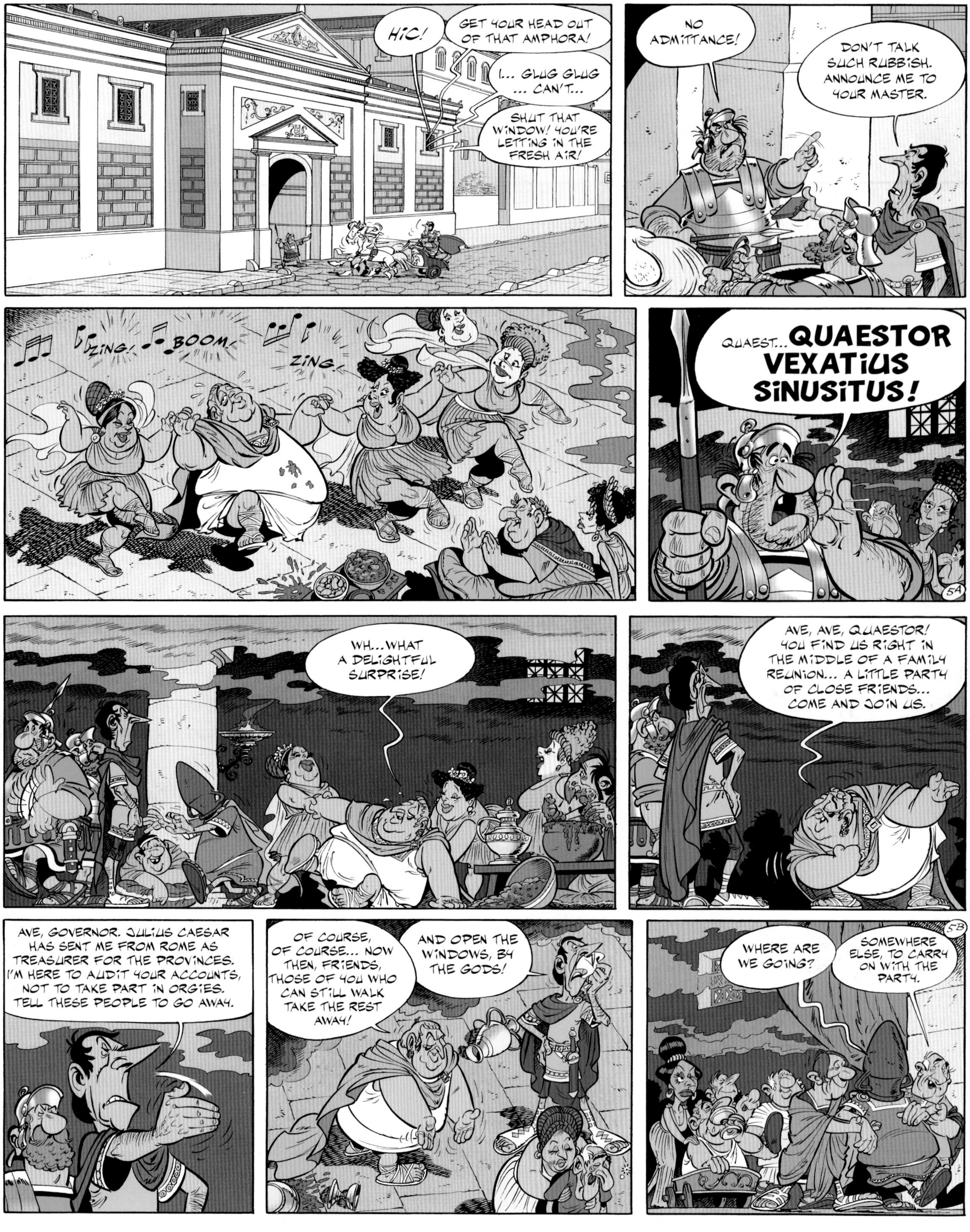
HIC!
GET YOUR HEAD OUT OF THAT AMPHORA!
I... GLUG GLUG ... CAN'T...
SHUT THAT WINDOW! YOU'RE LETTING IN THE FRESH AIR!
NO ADMITTANCE!
DON'T TALK SUCH RUBBISH. ANNOUNCE ME TO YOUR MASTER.
ZING!
BOOM!
ZING!
QUAEST... QUAESTOR VEXATIUS SINUSITUS!
WH... WHAT A DELIGHTFUL SURPRISE!
AVE, AVE, QUAESTOR! YOU FIND US RIGHT IN THE MIDDLE OF A FAMILY REUNION... A LITTLE PARTY OF CLOSE FRIENDS... COME AND JOIN US.
AVE, GOVERNOR. JULIUS CAESAR HAS SENT ME FROM ROME AS TREASURER FOR THE PROVINCES. I'M HERE TO AUDIT YOUR ACCOUNTS, NOT TO TAKE PART IN ORGIES. TELL THESE PEOPLE TO GO AWAY.
OF COURSE, OF COURSE... NOW THEN, FRIENDS, THOSE OF YOU WHO CAN STILL WALK TAKE THE REST AWAY!
AND OPEN THE WINDOWS, BY THE GODS!
WHERE ARE WE GOING?
SOMEWHERE ELSE, TO CARRY ON WITH THE PARTY.

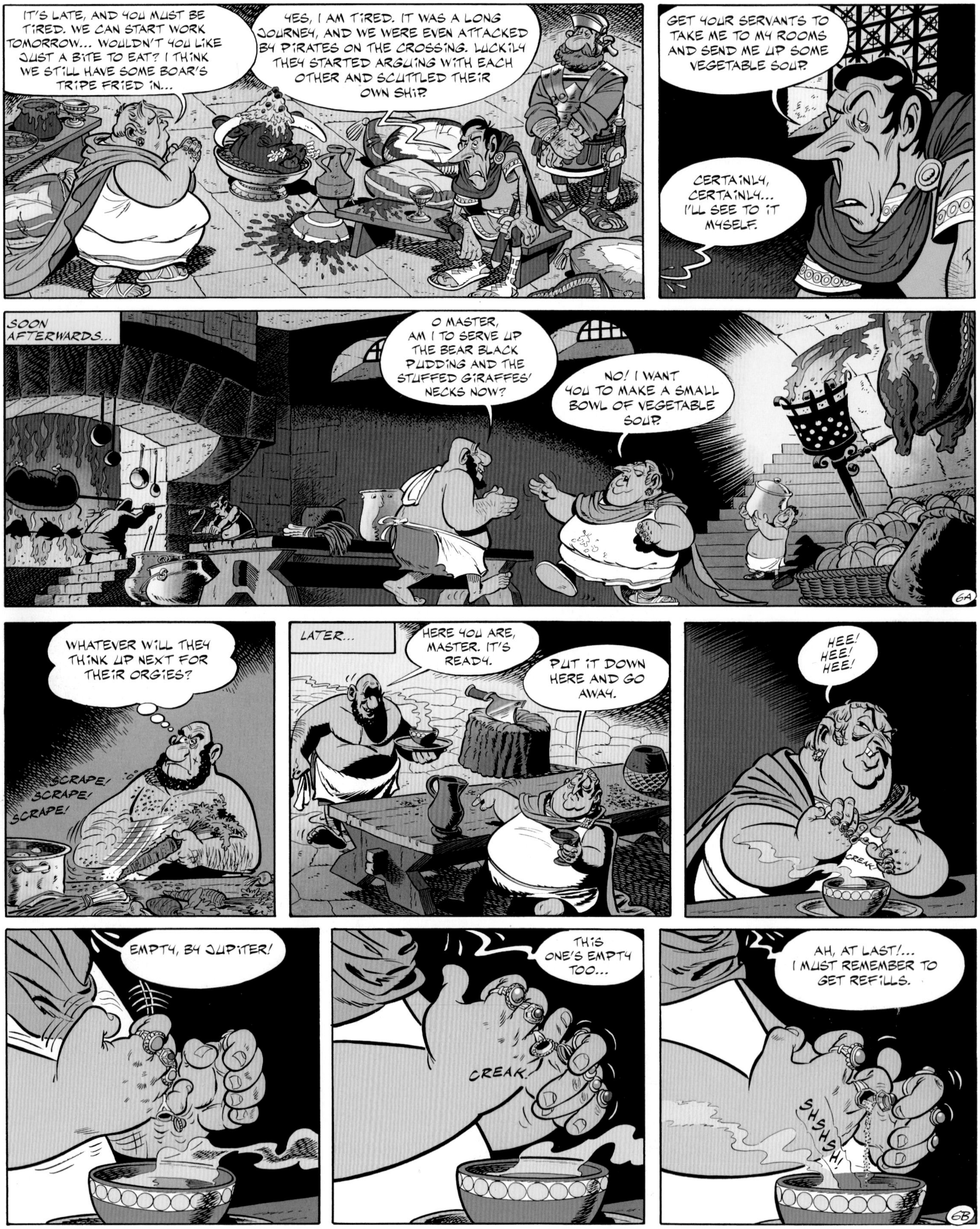
IT'S LATE, AND YOU MUST BE TIRED. WE CAN START WORK TOMORROW... WOULDN'T YOU LIKE JUST A BITE TO EAT? I THINK WE STILL HAVE SOME BOAR'S TRIPE FRIED IN...
YES, I AM TIRED. IT WAS A LONG JOURNEY, AND WE WERE EVEN ATTACKED BY PIRATES ON THE CROSSING. LUCKILY THEY STARTED ARGUING WITH EACH OTHER AND SCUTTLED THEIR OWN SHIP.
GET YOUR SERVANTS TO TAKE ME TO MY ROOMS AND SEND ME UP SOME VEGETABLE SOUP.
CERTAINLY, CERTAINLY... I'LL SEE TO IT MYSELF.
SOON AFTERWARDS...
O MASTER, AM I TO SERVE UP THE BEAR BLACK PUDDING AND THE STUFFED GIRAFFES' NECKS NOW?
NO! I WANT YOU TO MAKE A SMALL BOWL OF VEGETABLE SOUP.
WHATEVER WILL THEY THINK UP NEXT FOR THEIR ORGIES?
SCRAPE! SCRAPE! SCRAPE!
LATER...
HERE YOU ARE, MASTER. IT'S READY.
PUT IT DOWN HERE AND GO AWAY.
HEE! HEE! HEE!
CREAK!
EMPTY, BY JUPITER!
THIS ONE'S EMPTY TOO...
CREAK
AH, AT LAST!... I MUST REMEMBER TO GET REFILLS.
SHSHSH!

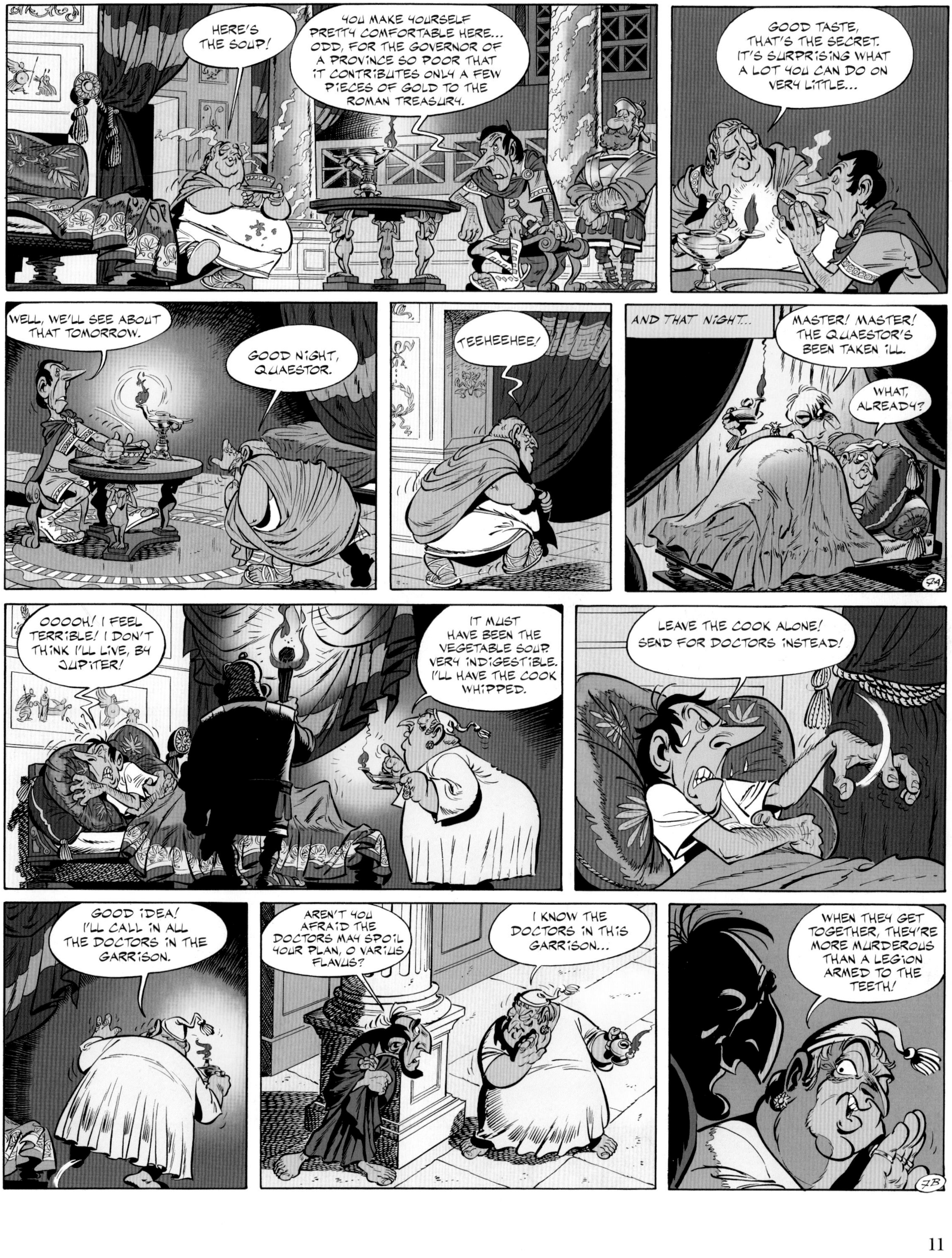
HERE'S THE SOUP!
YOU MAKE YOURSELF PRETTY COMFORTABLE HERE... ODD, FOR THE GOVERNOR OF A PROVINCE SO POOR THAT IT CONTRIBUTES ONLY A FEW PIECES OF GOLD TO THE ROMAN TREASURY.
GOOD TASTE, THAT'S THE SECRET. IT'S SURPRISING WHAT A LOT YOU CAN DO ON VERY LITTLE...
WELL, WE'LL SEE ABOUT THAT TOMORROW.
GOOD NIGHT, QUAESTOR.
TEEHEEHEE!
AND THAT NIGHT...
MASTER! MASTER! THE QUAESTOR'S BEEN TAKEN ILL.
WHAT, ALREADY?
OOOOH! I FEEL TERRIBLE! I DON'T THINK I'LL LIVE, BY JUPITER!
IT MUST HAVE BEEN THE VEGETABLE SOUP. VERY INDIGESTIBLE. I'LL HAVE THE COOK WHIPPED.
LEAVE THE COOK ALONE! SEND FOR DOCTORS INSTEAD!
GOOD IDEA! I'LL CALL IN ALL THE DOCTORS IN THE GARRISON.
AREN'T YOU AFRAID THE DOCTORS MAY SPOIL YOUR PLAN, O VARIUS FLAVUS?
I KNOW THE DOCTORS IN THIS GARRISON...
WHEN THEY GET TOGETHER, THEY'RE MORE MURDEROUS THAN A LEGION ARMED TO THE TEETH!
7A
7B

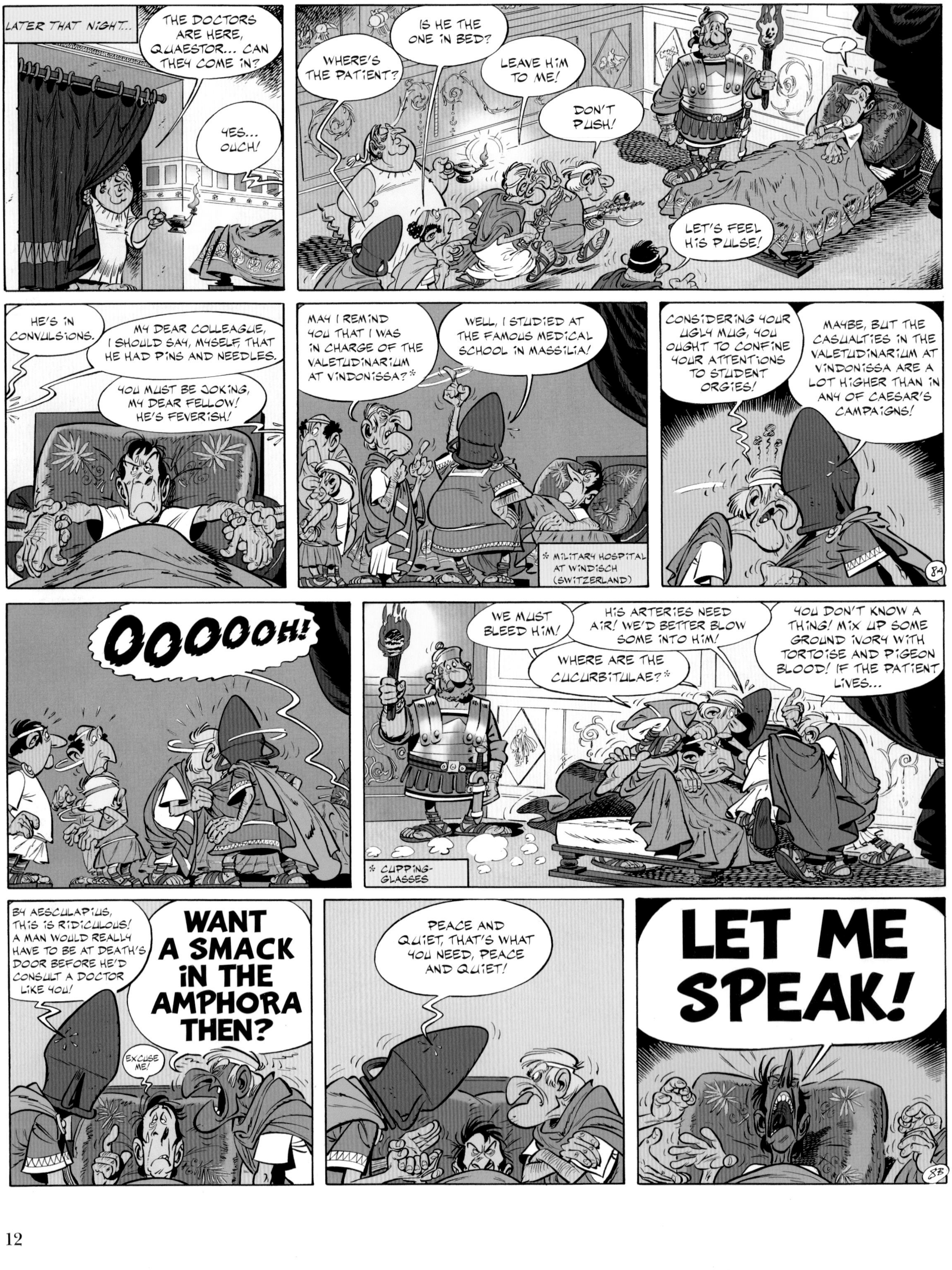

LATER THAT NIGHT...
THE DOCTORS ARE HERE, QUAESTOR... CAN THEY COME IN?
YES... OUCH!
WHERE'S THE PATIENT?
IS HE THE ONE IN BED?
LEAVE HIM TO ME!
DON'T PUSH!
!
LET'S FEEL HIS PULSE!
HE'S IN CONVULSIONS.
MY DEAR COLLEAGUE, I SHOULD SAY, MYSELF, THAT HE HAD PINS AND NEEDLES.
YOU MUST BE JOKING, MY DEAR FELLOW! HE'S FEVERISH!
MAY I REMIND YOU THAT I WAS IN CHARGE OF THE VALETUDINARIUM AT VINDONISSA?*
WELL, I STUDIED AT THE FAMOUS MEDICAL SCHOOL IN MASSILIA!
* MILITARY HOSPITAL AT WINDISCH (SWITZERLAND)
CONSIDERING YOUR UGLY MUG, YOU OUGHT TO CONFINE YOUR ATTENTIONS TO STUDENT ORGIES!
MAYBE, BUT THE CASUALTIES IN THE VALETUDINARIUM AT VINDONISSA ARE A LOT HIGHER THAN IN ANY OF CAESAR'S CAMPAIGNS!
OOOOOH!
WE MUST BLEED HIM!
HIS ARTERIES NEED AIR! WE'D BETTER BLOW SOME INTO HIM!
WHERE ARE THE CUCURBITULAE?*
YOU DON'T KNOW A THING! MIX UP SOME GROUND IVORY WITH TORTOISE AND PIGEON BLOOD! IF THE PATIENT LIVES...
* CUPPING-GLASSES
BY AESCULAPIUS, THIS IS RIDICULOUS! A MAN WOULD REALLY HAVE TO BE AT DEATH'S DOOR BEFORE HE'D CONSULT A DOCTOR LIKE YOU!
WANT A SMACK IN THE AMPHORA THEN?
EXCUSE ME!
PEACE AND QUIET, THAT'S WHAT YOU NEED, PEACE AND QUIET!
LET ME SPEAK!

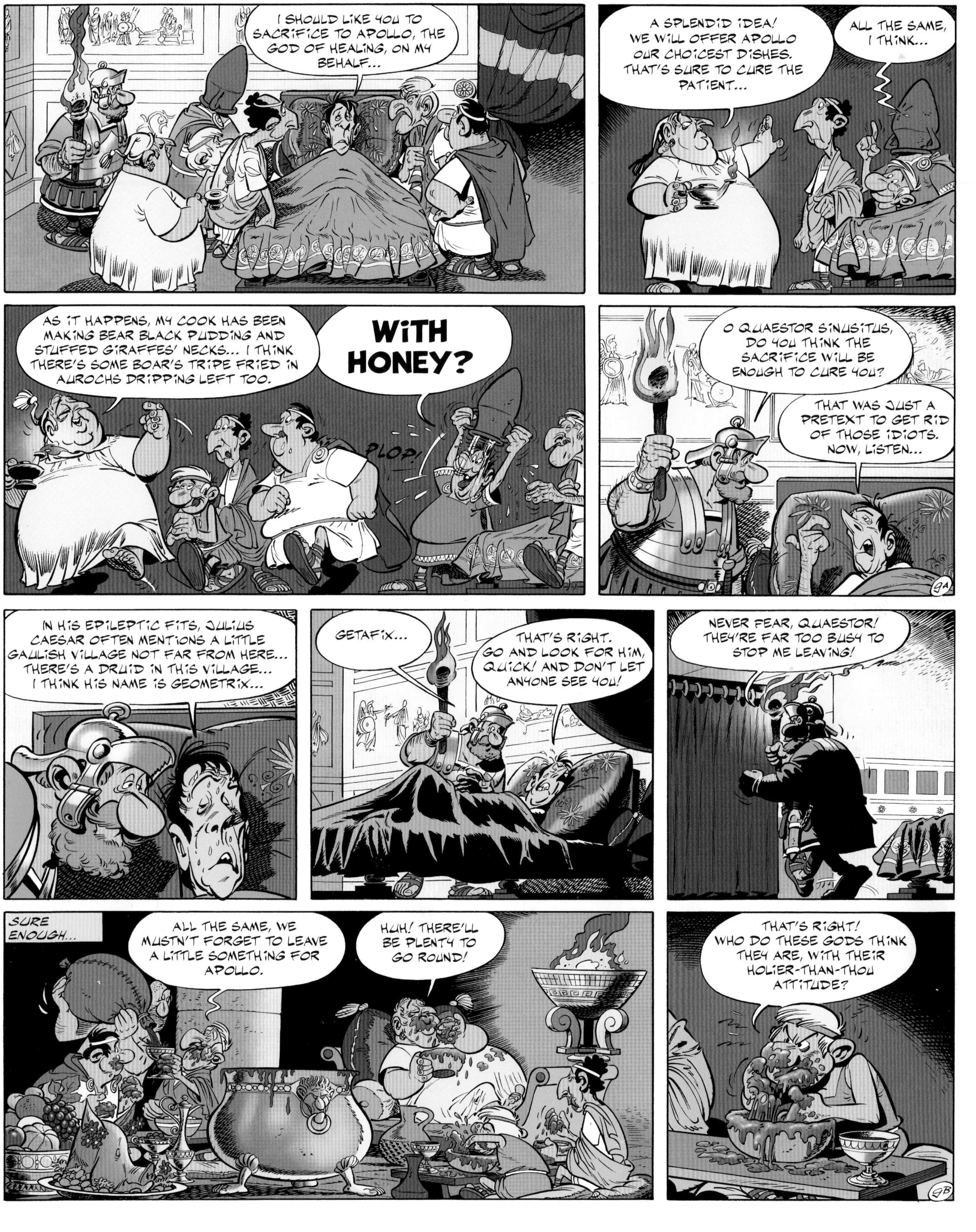
I SHOULD LIKE YOU TO SACRIFICE TO APOLLO, THE GOD OF HEALING, ON MY BEHALF...
A SPLENDID IDEA! WE WILL OFFER APOLLO OUR CHOICEST DISHES. THAT'S SURE TO CURE THE PATIENT...
ALL THE SAME, I THINK...
AS IT HAPPENS, MY COOK HAS BEEN MAKING BEAR BLACK PUDDING AND STUFFED GIRAFFES' NECKS... I THINK THERE'S SOME BOAR'S TRIPE FRIED IN AUROCHS DRIPPING LEFT TOO.
WITH HONEY?
PLOP!
O QUAESTOR SINUSITUS, DO YOU THINK THE SACRIFICE WILL BE ENOUGH TO CURE YOU?
THAT WAS JUST A PRETEXT TO GET RID OF THOSE IDIOTS. NOW, LISTEN...
IN HIS EPILEPTIC FITS, JULIUS CAESAR OFTEN MENTIONS A LITTLE GAULISH VILLAGE NOT FAR FROM HERE... THERE'S A DRUID IN THIS VILLAGE... I THINK HIS NAME IS GEOMETRIX...
GETAFIX...
THAT'S RIGHT. GO AND LOOK FOR HIM, QUICK! AND DON'T LET ANYONE SEE YOU!
NEVER FEAR, QUAESTOR! THEY'RE FAR TOO BUSY TO STOP ME LEAVING!
SURE ENOUGH...
ALL THE SAME, WE MUSTN'T FORGET TO LEAVE A LITTLE SOMETHING FOR APOLLO.
HUH! THERE'LL BE PLENTY TO GO ROUND!
THAT'S RIGHT! WHO DO THESE GODS THINK THEY ARE, WITH THEIR HOLIER-THAN-THOU ATTITUDE?

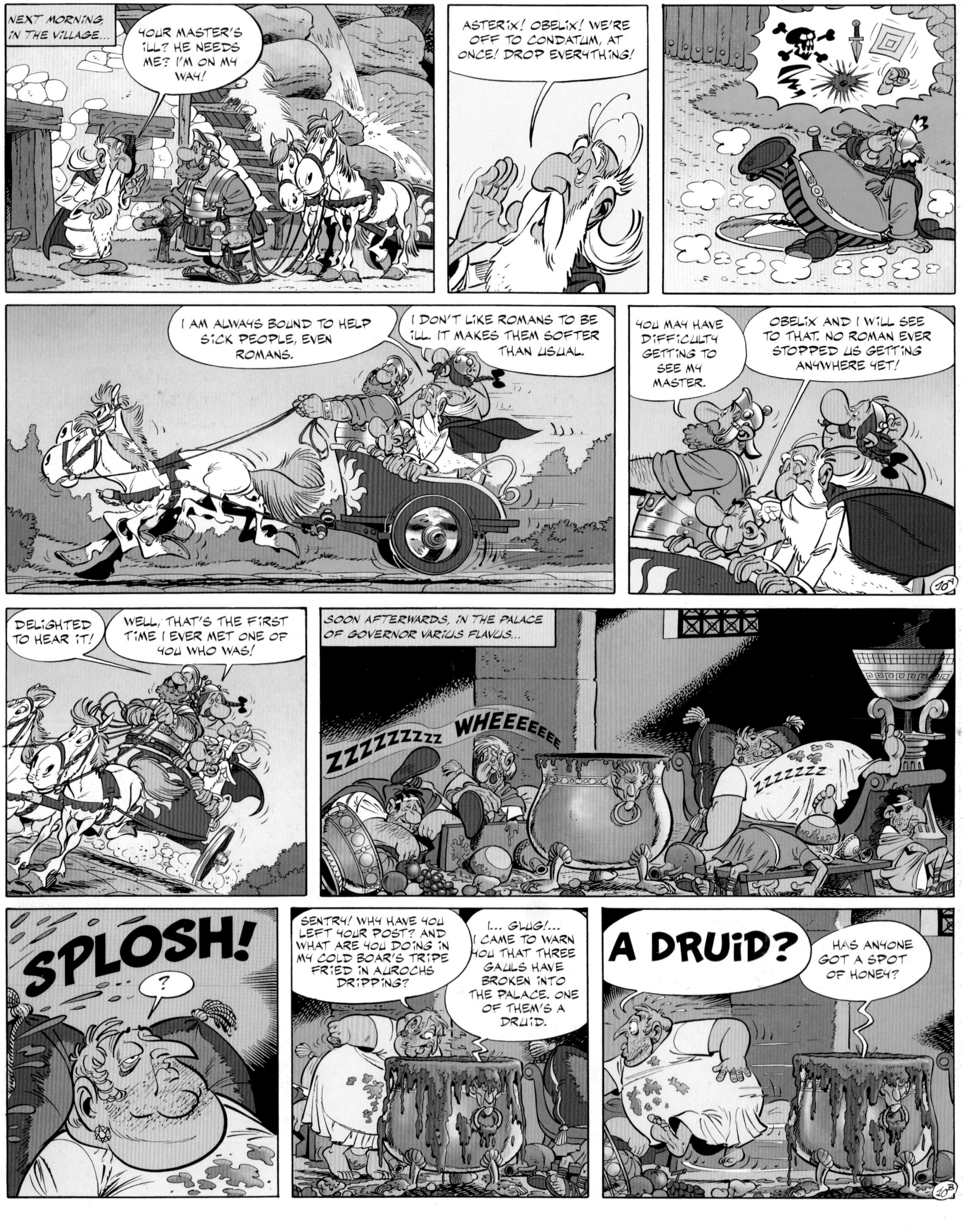
NEXT MORNING, IN THE VILLAGE...
YOUR MASTER'S ILL? HE NEEDS ME? I'M ON MY WAY!
ASTERIX! OBELIX! WE'RE OFF TO CONDATUM, AT ONCE! DROP EVERYTHING!
I AM ALWAYS BOUND TO HELP SICK PEOPLE, EVEN ROMANS.
I DON'T LIKE ROMANS TO BE ILL. IT MAKES THEM SOFTER THAN USUAL.
YOU MAY HAVE DIFFICULTY GETTING TO SEE MY MASTER.
OBELIX AND I WILL SEE TO THAT. NO ROMAN EVER STOPPED US GETTING ANYWHERE YET!
DELIGHTED TO HEAR IT!
WELL, THAT'S THE FIRST TIME I EVER MET ONE OF YOU WHO WAS!
SOON AFTERWARDS, IN THE PALACE OF GOVERNOR VARIUS FLAVUS...
ZZZZZZZzz
WHEEEEEEE
ZZZZZZZ
SPLOSH!
?
SENTRY! WHY HAVE YOU LEFT YOUR POST? AND WHAT ARE YOU DOING IN MY COLD BOAR'S TRIPE FRIED IN AUROCHS DRIPPING?
I... GLUG!... I CAME TO WARN YOU THAT THREE GAULS HAVE BROKEN INTO THE PALACE. ONE OF THEM'S A DRUID.
A DRUID?
HAS ANYONE GOT A SPOT OF HONEY?

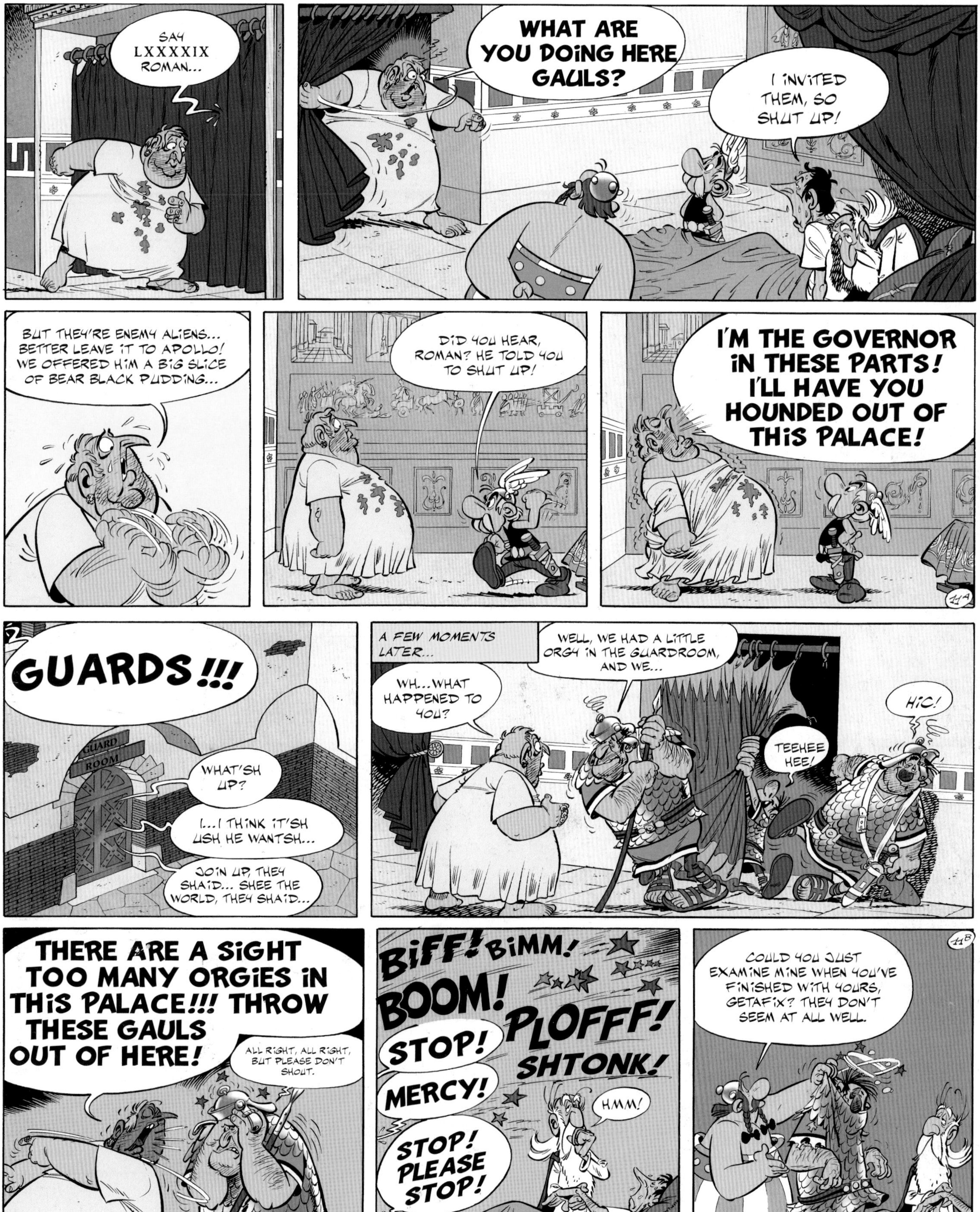
SAY LXXXXIX ROMAN...
WHAT ARE YOU DOING HERE GAULS?
I INVITED THEM, SO SHUT UP!
BUT THEY'RE ENEMY ALIENS... BETTER LEAVE IT TO APOLLO! WE OFFERED HIM A BIG SLICE OF BEAR BLACK PUDDING...
DID YOU HEAR, ROMAN? HE TOLD YOU TO SHUT UP!
I'M THE GOVERNOR IN THESE PARTS! I'LL HAVE YOU HOUNDED OUT OF THIS PALACE!
GUARDS!!!
GUARD ROOM
WHAT'SH UP?
I... I THINK IT'SH USH HE WANTSH...
JOIN UP, THEY SHAID... SHEE THE WORLD, THEY SHAID...
A FEW MOMENTS LATER...
WELL, WE HAD A LITTLE ORGY IN THE GUARDROOM, AND WE...
WH... WHAT HAPPENED TO YOU?
HIC!
TEEHEE HEE!
THERE ARE A SIGHT TOO MANY ORGIES IN THIS PALACE!!! THROW THESE GAULS OUT OF HERE!
ALL RIGHT, ALL RIGHT, BUT PLEASE DON'T SHOUT.
BIFF! BIMM!
BOOM!
PLOFFF!
STOP!
SHTONK!
MERCY!
HMM!
STOP! PLEASE STOP!
COULD YOU JUST EXAMINE MINE WHEN YOU'VE FINISHED WITH YOURS, GETAFIX? THEY DON'T SEEM AT ALL WELL.

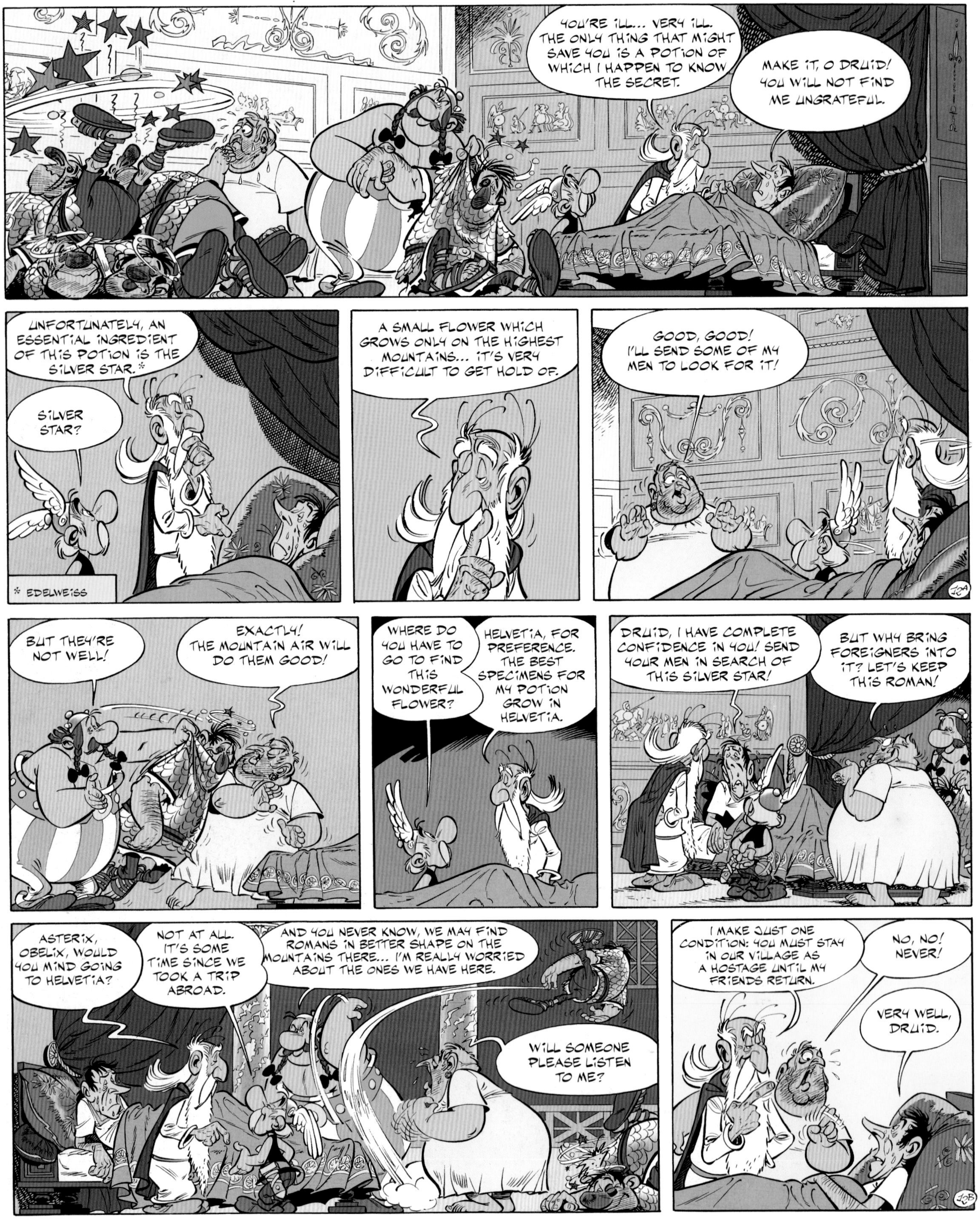

YOU'RE ILL... VERY ILL. THE ONLY THING THAT MIGHT SAVE YOU IS A POTION OF WHICH I HAPPEN TO KNOW THE SECRET.
MAKE IT, O DRUID! YOU WILL NOT FIND ME UNGRATEFUL.
UNFORTUNATELY, AN ESSENTIAL INGREDIENT OF THIS POTION IS THE SILVER STAR.*
SILVER STAR?
* EDELWEISS
A SMALL FLOWER WHICH GROWS ONLY ON THE HIGHEST MOUNTAINS... IT'S VERY DIFFICULT TO GET HOLD OF.
GOOD, GOOD! I'LL SEND SOME OF MY MEN TO LOOK FOR IT!
BUT THEY'RE NOT WELL!
EXACTLY! THE MOUNTAIN AIR WILL DO THEM GOOD!
WHERE DO YOU HAVE TO GO TO FIND THIS WONDERFUL FLOWER?
HELVETIA, FOR PREFERENCE. THE BEST SPECIMENS FOR MY POTION GROW IN HELVETIA.
DRUID, I HAVE COMPLETE CONFIDENCE IN YOU! SEND YOUR MEN IN SEARCH OF THIS SILVER STAR!
BUT WHY BRING FOREIGNERS INTO IT? LET'S KEEP THIS ROMAN!
ASTERIX, OBELIX, WOULD YOU MIND GOING TO HELVETIA?
NOT AT ALL. IT'S SOME TIME SINCE WE TOOK A TRIP ABROAD.
AND YOU NEVER KNOW, WE MAY FIND ROMANS IN BETTER SHAPE ON THE MOUNTAINS THERE... I'M REALLY WORRIED ABOUT THE ONES WE HAVE HERE.
WILL SOMEONE PLEASE LISTEN TO ME?
I MAKE JUST ONE CONDITION: YOU MUST STAY IN OUR VILLAGE AS A HOSTAGE UNTIL MY FRIENDS RETURN.
NO, NO! NEVER!
VERY WELL, DRUID.

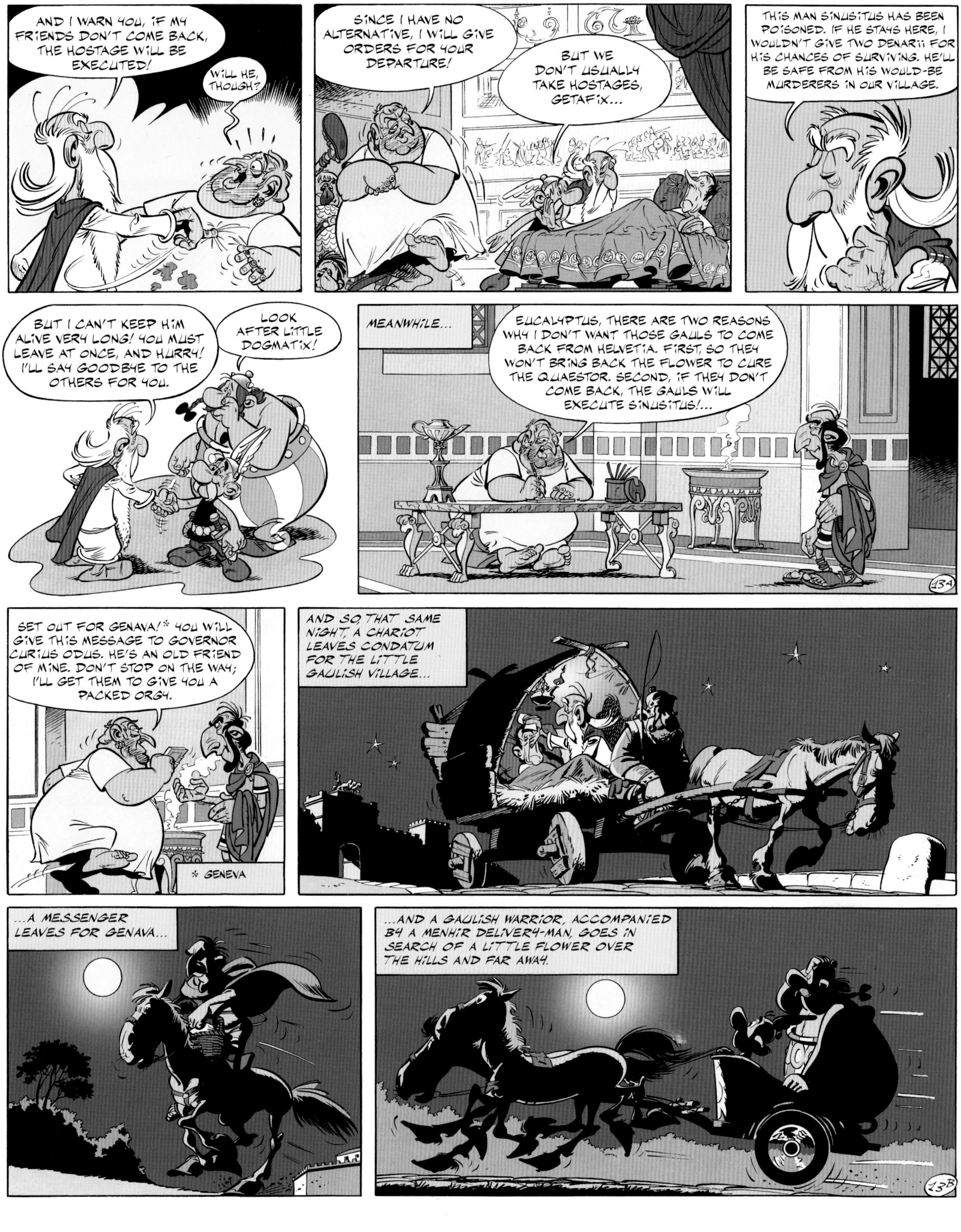
AND I WARN YOU, IF MY FRIENDS DON'T COME BACK, THE HOSTAGE WILL BE EXECUTED!
WILL HE, THOUGH?
SINCE I HAVE NO ALTERNATIVE, I WILL GIVE ORDERS FOR YOUR DEPARTURE!
BUT WE DON'T USUALLY TAKE HOSTAGES, GETAFIX...
THIS MAN SINUSITUS HAS BEEN POISONED. IF HE STAYS HERE, I WOULDN'T GIVE TWO DENARII FOR HIS CHANCES OF SURVIVING. HE'LL BE SAFE FROM HIS WOULD-BE MURDERERS IN OUR VILLAGE.
BUT I CAN'T KEEP HIM ALIVE VERY LONG! YOU MUST LEAVE AT ONCE, AND HURRY! I'LL SAY GOODBYE TO THE OTHERS FOR YOU.
LOOK AFTER LITTLE DOGMATIX!
MEANWHILE...
EUCALYPTUS, THERE ARE TWO REASONS WHY I DON'T WANT THOSE GAULS TO COME BACK FROM HELVETIA. FIRST, SO THEY WON'T BRING BACK THE FLOWER TO CURE THE QUAESTOR. SECOND, IF THEY DON'T COME BACK, THE GAULS WILL EXECUTE SINUSITUS!...
13A
SET OUT FOR GENAVA!* YOU WILL GIVE THIS MESSAGE TO GOVERNOR CURIUS ODUS. HE'S AN OLD FRIEND OF MINE. DON'T STOP ON THE WAY; I'LL GET THEM TO GIVE YOU A PACKED ORGY.
* GENEVA
AND SO, THAT SAME NIGHT, A CHARIOT LEAVES CONDATUM FOR THE LITTLE GAULISH VILLAGE...
...A MESSENGER LEAVES FOR GENAVA...
...AND A GAULISH WARRIOR, ACCOMPANIED BY A MENHIR DELIVERY-MAN, GOES IN SEARCH OF A LITTLE FLOWER OVER THE HILLS AND FAR AWAY.
13B

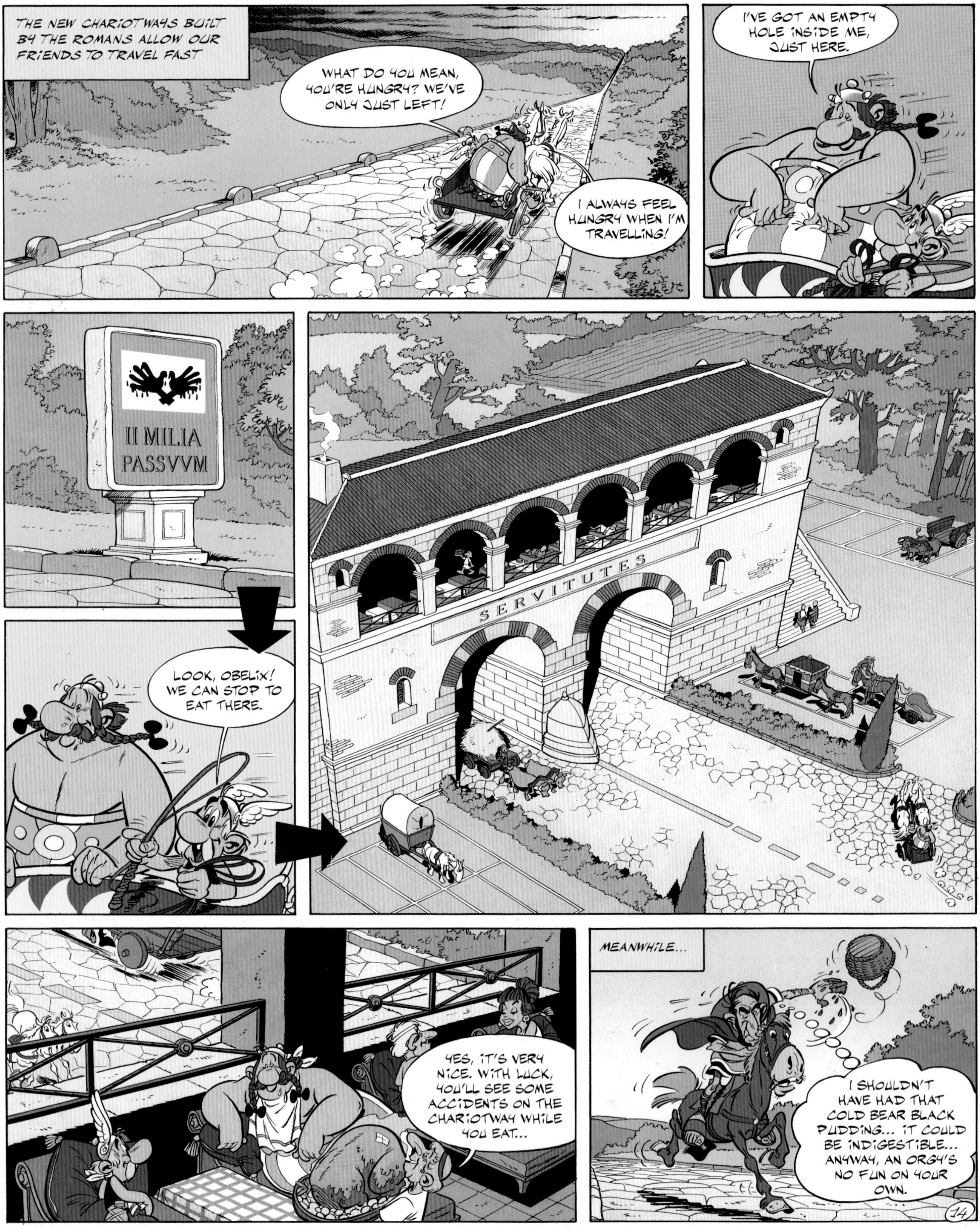
THE NEW CHARIOTWAYS BUILT BY THE ROMANS ALLOW OUR FRIENDS TO TRAVEL FAST
WHAT DO YOU MEAN, YOU'RE HUNGRY? WE'VE ONLY JUST LEFT!
I ALWAYS FEEL HUNGRY WHEN I'M TRAVELLING!
I'VE GOT AN EMPTY HOLE INSIDE ME, JUST HERE.
II MILIA PASSVVM
LOOK, OBELIX! WE CAN STOP TO EAT THERE.
SERVITUTES
YES, IT'S VERY NICE. WITH LUCK, YOU'LL SEE SOME ACCIDENTS ON THE CHARIOTWAY WHILE YOU EAT...
MEANWHILE...
I SHOULDN'T HAVE HAD THAT COLD BEAR BLACK PUDDING... IT COULD BE INDIGESTIBLE... ANYWAY, AN ORGY'S NO FUN ON YOUR OWN.
14

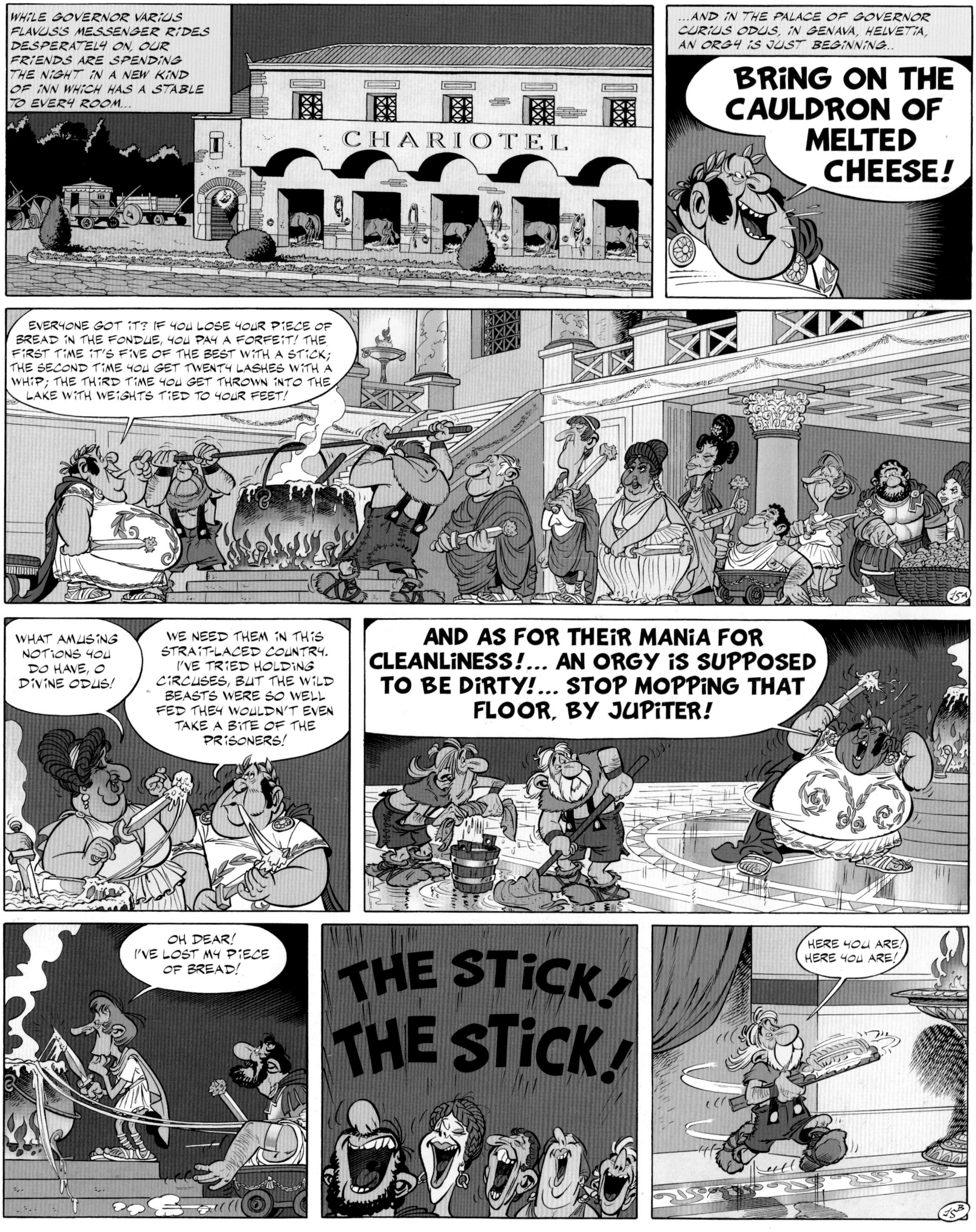
WHILE GOVERNOR VARIUS FLAVUS'S MESSENGER RIDES DESPERATELY ON, OUR FRIENDS ARE SPENDING THE NIGHT IN A NEW KIND OF INN WHICH HAS A STABLE TO EVERY ROOM...
CHARIOTEL
...AND IN THE PALACE OF GOVERNOR CURIUS ODUS, IN GENAVA, HELVETIA, AN ORGY IS JUST BEGINNING...
BRING ON THE CAULDRON OF MELTED CHEESE!
EVERYONE GOT IT? IF YOU LOSE YOUR PIECE OF BREAD IN THE FONDUE, YOU PAY A FORFEIT! THE FIRST TIME IT'S FIVE OF THE BEST WITH A STICK; THE SECOND TIME YOU GET TWENTY LASHES WITH A WHIP; THE THIRD TIME YOU GET THROWN INTO THE LAKE WITH WEIGHTS TIED TO YOUR FEET!
WHAT AMUSING NOTIONS YOU DO HAVE, O DIVINE ODUS!
WE NEED THEM IN THIS STRAIT-LACED COUNTRY. I'VE TRIED HOLDING CIRCUSES, BUT THE WILD BEASTS WERE SO WELL FED THEY WOULDN'T EVEN TAKE A BITE OF THE PRISONERS!
AND AS FOR THEIR MANIA FOR CLEANLINESS!... AN ORGY IS SUPPOSED TO BE DIRTY!... STOP MOPPING THAT FLOOR, BY JUPITER!
OH DEAR! I'VE LOST MY PIECE OF BREAD!
THE STICK! THE STICK!
HERE YOU ARE! HERE YOU ARE!

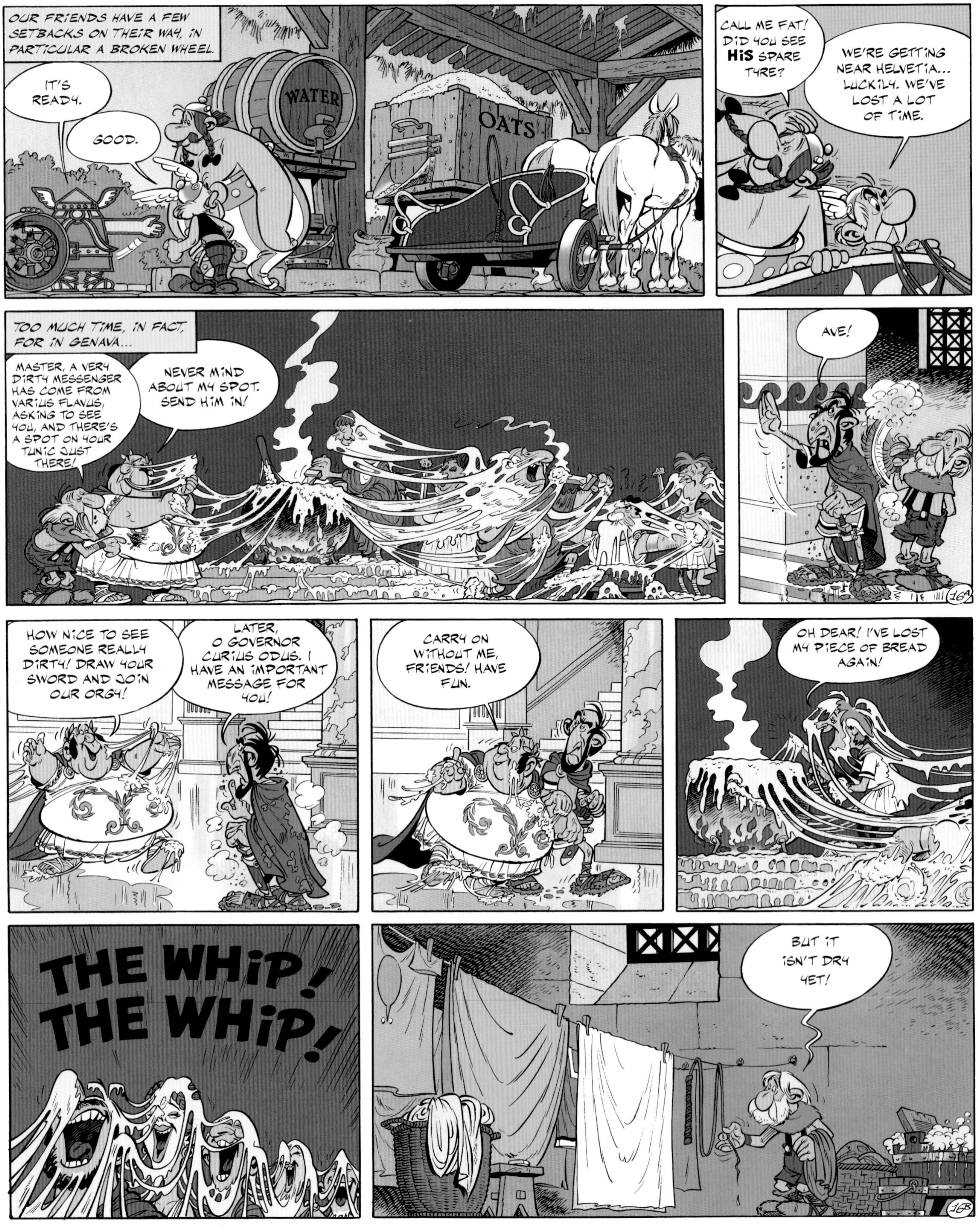
OUR FRIENDS HAVE A FEW SETBACKS ON THEIR WAY, IN PARTICULAR A BROKEN WHEEL.
IT'S READY.
GOOD.
WATER
OATS
CALL ME FAT! DID YOU SEE HIS SPARE TYRE?
WE'RE GETTING NEAR HELVETIA... LUCKILY. WE'VE LOST A LOT OF TIME.
TOO MUCH TIME, IN FACT, FOR IN GENAVA...
MASTER, A VERY DIRTY MESSENGER HAS COME FROM VARIUS FLAVUS, ASKING TO SEE YOU, AND THERE'S A SPOT ON YOUR TUNIC JUST THERE!
NEVER MIND ABOUT MY SPOT. SEND HIM IN!
AVE!
HOW NICE TO SEE SOMEONE REALLY DIRTY! DRAW YOUR SWORD AND JOIN OUR ORGY!
LATER, O GOVERNOR CURIUS ODUS. I HAVE AN IMPORTANT MESSAGE FOR YOU!
CARRY ON WITHOUT ME, FRIENDS! HAVE FUN.
OH DEAR! I'VE LOST MY PIECE OF BREAD AGAIN!
THE WHIP! THE WHIP!
BUT IT ISN'T DRY YET!

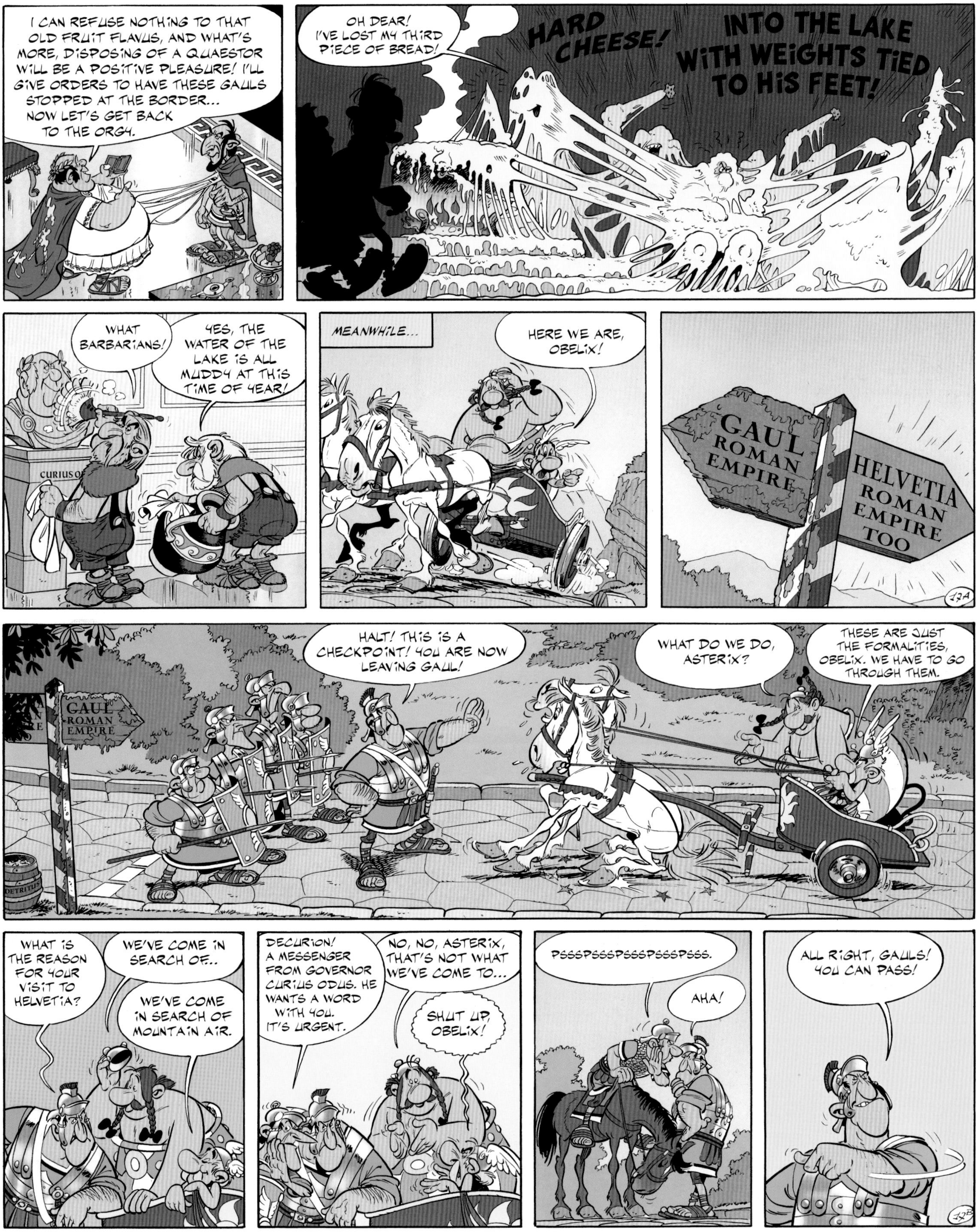
I CAN REFUSE NOTHING TO THAT OLD FRUIT FLAVUS, AND WHAT'S MORE, DISPOSING OF A QUAESTOR WILL BE A POSITIVE PLEASURE! I'LL GIVE ORDERS TO HAVE THESE GAULS STOPPED AT THE BORDER... NOW LET'S GET BACK TO THE ORGY.
OH DEAR! I'VE LOST MY THIRD PIECE OF BREAD!
HARD CHEESE!
INTO THE LAKE WITH WEIGHTS TIED TO HIS FEET!
WHAT BARBARIANS!
YES, THE WATER OF THE LAKE IS ALL MUDDY AT THIS TIME OF YEAR!
CURIUS O
MEANWHILE...
HERE WE ARE, OBELIX!
GAUL ROMAN EMPIRE
HELVETIA ROMAN EMPIRE TOO
HALT! THIS IS A CHECKPOINT! YOU ARE NOW LEAVING GAUL!
WHAT DO WE DO, ASTERIX?
THESE ARE JUST THE FORMALITIES, OBELIX. WE HAVE TO GO THROUGH THEM.
GAUL ROMAN EMPIRE
WHAT IS THE REASON FOR YOUR VISIT TO HELVETIA?
WE'VE COME IN SEARCH OF..
WE'VE COME IN SEARCH OF MOUNTAIN AIR.
DECURION! A MESSENGER FROM GOVERNOR CURIUS ODUS. HE WANTS A WORD WITH YOU. IT'S URGENT.
NO, NO, ASTERIX, THAT'S NOT WHAT WE'VE COME TO...
SHUT UP, OBELIX!
PSSSPSSSPSSSPSSSPSSS.
AHA!
ALL RIGHT, GAULS! YOU CAN PASS!

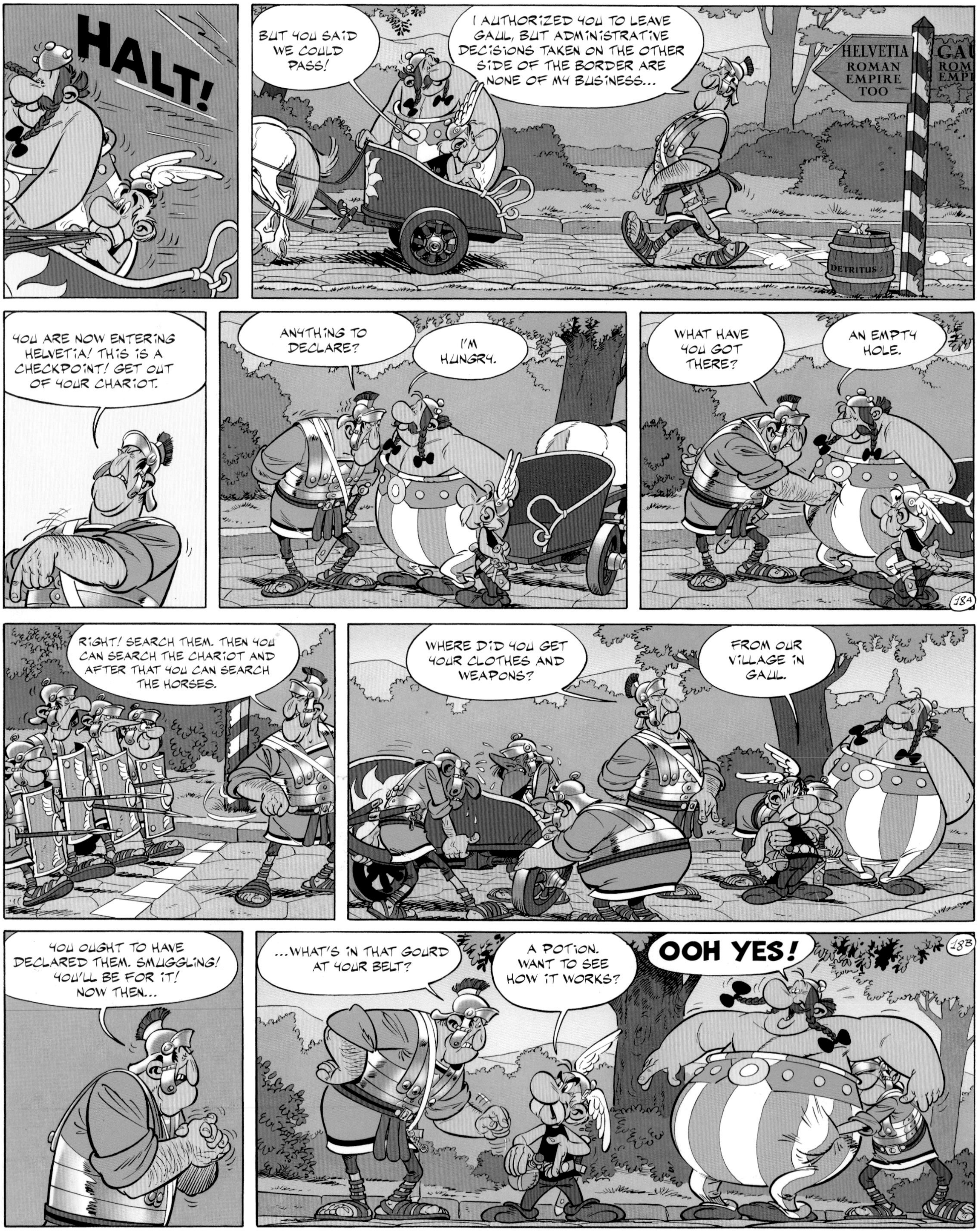
HALT!
BUT YOU SAID WE COULD PASS!
I AUTHORIZED YOU TO LEAVE GAUL, BUT ADMINISTRATIVE DECISIONS TAKEN ON THE OTHER SIDE OF THE BORDER ARE NONE OF MY BUSINESS...
HELVETIA ROMAN EMPIRE TOO
DETRITUS
YOU ARE NOW ENTERING HELVETIA! THIS IS A CHECKPOINT! GET OUT OF YOUR CHARIOT.
ANYTHING TO DECLARE?
I'M HUNGRY.
WHAT HAVE YOU GOT THERE?
AN EMPTY HOLE.
RIGHT! SEARCH THEM. THEN YOU CAN SEARCH THE CHARIOT AND AFTER THAT YOU CAN SEARCH THE HORSES.
WHERE DID YOU GET YOUR CLOTHES AND WEAPONS?
FROM OUR VILLAGE IN GAUL.
YOU OUGHT TO HAVE DECLARED THEM. SMUGGLING! YOU'LL BE FOR IT! NOW THEN...
...WHAT'S IN THAT GOURD AT YOUR BELT?
A POTION. WANT TO SEE HOW IT WORKS?
OOH YES!

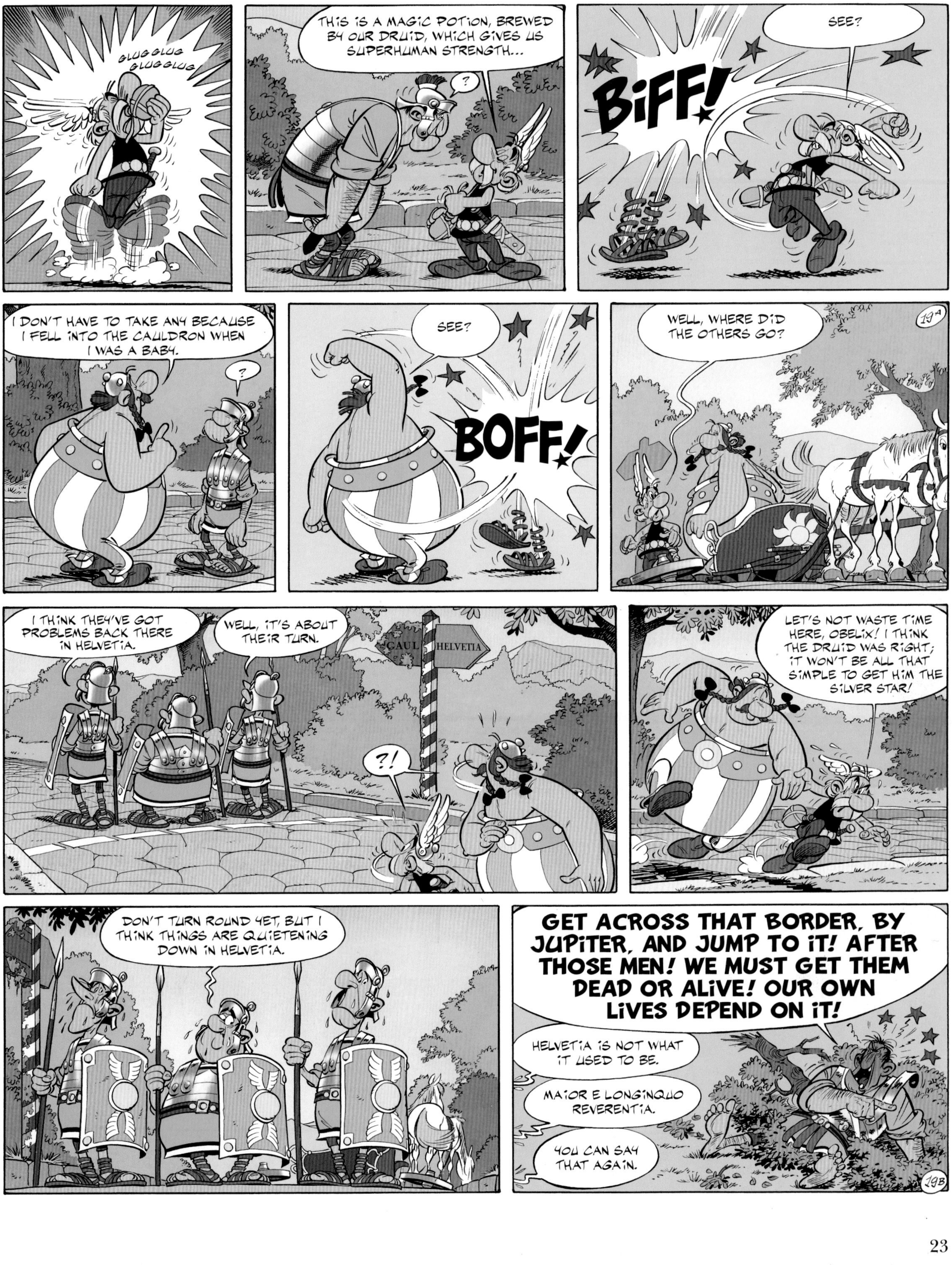
GLUGGLUG GLUGGLUG
THIS IS A MAGIC POTION, BREWED BY OUR DRUID, WHICH GIVES US SUPERHUMAN STRENGTH...
?
SEE?
BIFF!
I DON'T HAVE TO TAKE ANY BECAUSE I FELL INTO THE CAULDRON WHEN I WAS A BABY.
?
SEE?
BOFF!
WELL, WHERE DID THE OTHERS GO?
19A
I THINK THEY'VE GOT PROBLEMS BACK THERE IN HELVETIA.
WELL, IT'S ABOUT THEIR TURN.
GAUL
HELVETIA
?!
LET'S NOT WASTE TIME HERE, OBELIX! I THINK THE DRUID WAS RIGHT; IT WON'T BE ALL THAT SIMPLE TO GET HIM THE SILVER STAR!
DON'T TURN ROUND YET, BUT I THINK THINGS ARE QUIETENING DOWN IN HELVETIA.
GET ACROSS THAT BORDER, BY JUPITER, AND JUMP TO IT! AFTER THOSE MEN! WE MUST GET THEM DEAD OR ALIVE! OUR OWN LIVES DEPEND ON IT!
HELVETIA IS NOT WHAT IT USED TO BE.
MAIOR E LONGINQUO REVERENTIA.
YOU CAN SAY THAT AGAIN.
19B

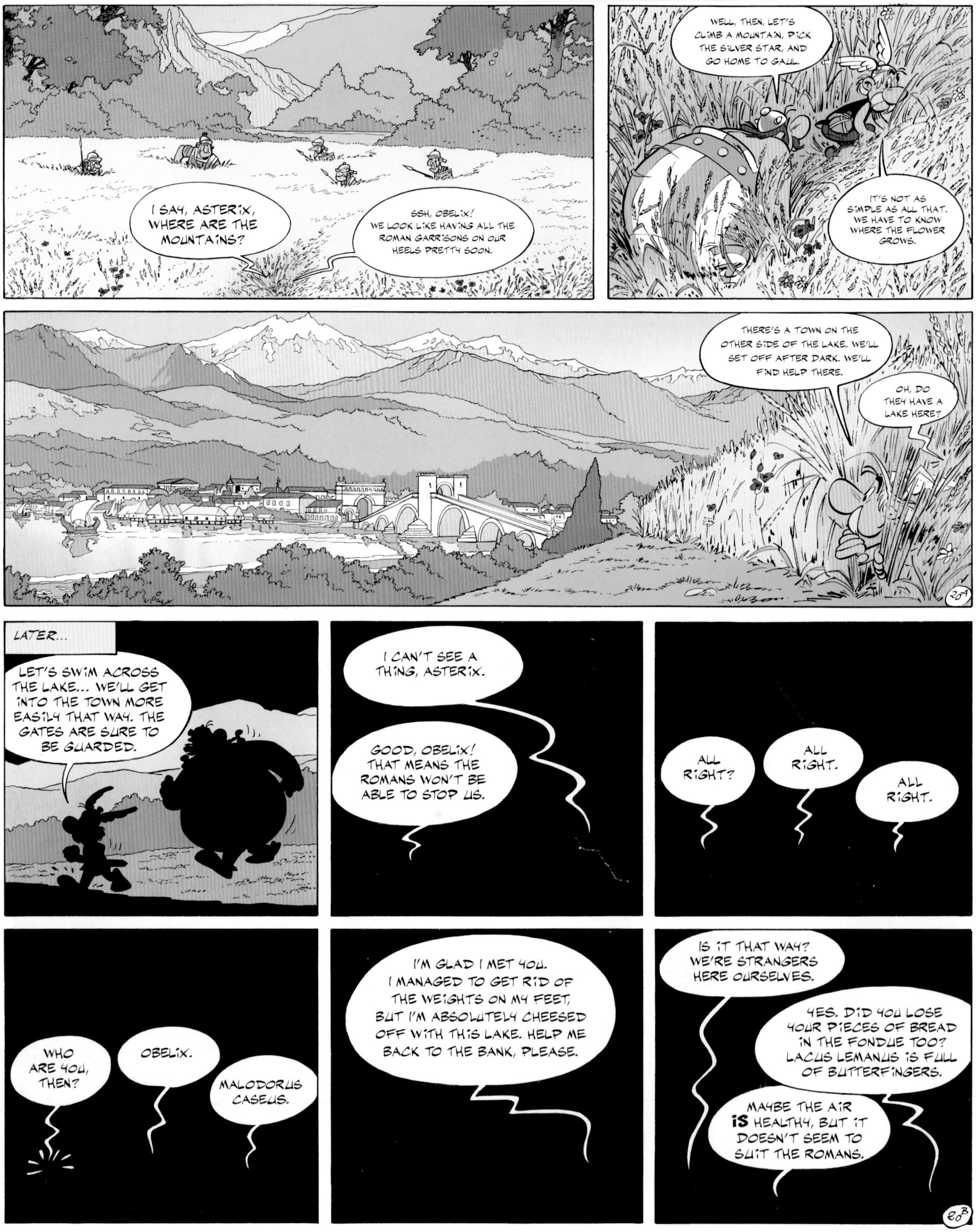
I SAY, ASTERIX, WHERE ARE THE MOUNTAINS?
SSH, OBELIX! WE LOOK LIKE HAVING ALL THE ROMAN GARRISONS ON OUR HEELS PRETTY SOON.
WELL, THEN, LET'S CLIMB A MOUNTAIN, PICK THE SILVER STAR, AND GO HOME TO GAUL.
IT'S NOT AS SIMPLE AS ALL THAT. WE HAVE TO KNOW WHERE THE FLOWER GROWS.
THERE'S A TOWN ON THE OTHER SIDE OF THE LAKE. WE'LL SET OFF AFTER DARK. WE'LL FIND HELP THERE.
OH, DO THEY HAVE A LAKE HERE?
LATER...
LET'S SWIM ACROSS THE LAKE... WE'LL GET INTO THE TOWN MORE EASILY THAT WAY. THE GATES ARE SURE TO BE GUARDED.
I CAN'T SEE A THING, ASTERIX.
GOOD, OBELIX! THAT MEANS THE ROMANS WON'T BE ABLE TO STOP US.
ALL RIGHT?
ALL RIGHT.
ALL RIGHT.
WHO ARE YOU, THEN?
OBELIX.
MALODORUS CASEUS.
I'M GLAD I MET YOU. I MANAGED TO GET RID OF THE WEIGHTS ON MY FEET, BUT I'M ABSOLUTELY CHEESED OFF WITH THIS LAKE. HELP ME BACK TO THE BANK, PLEASE.
IS IT THAT WAY? WE'RE STRANGERS HERE OURSELVES.
YES. DID YOU LOSE YOUR PIECES OF BREAD IN THE FONDUE TOO? LACUS LEMANUS IS FULL OF BUTTERFINGERS.
MAYBE THE AIR **IS** HEALTHY, BUT IT DOESN'T SEEM TO SUIT THE ROMANS.

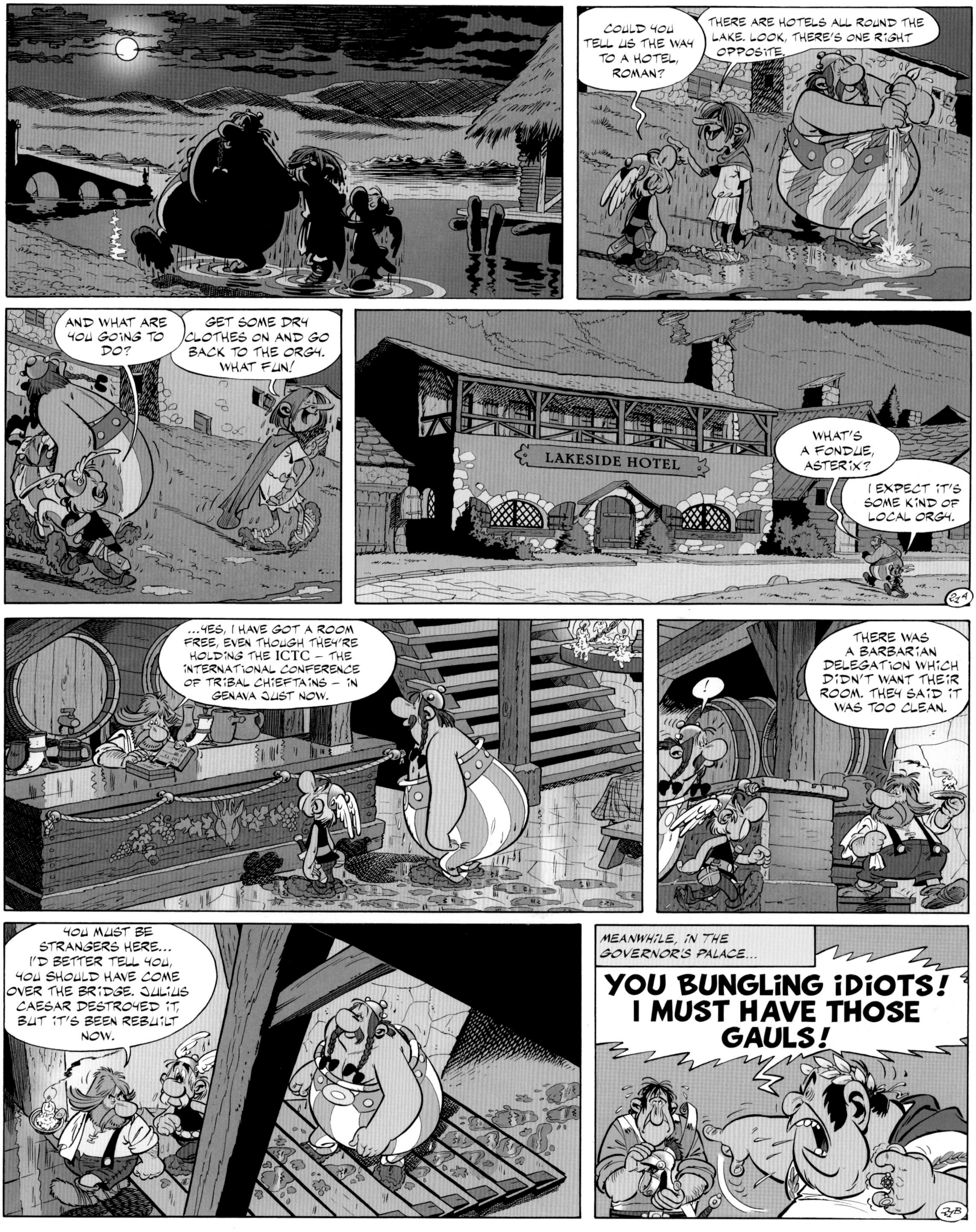
COULD YOU TELL US THE WAY TO A HOTEL, ROMAN?
THERE ARE HOTELS ALL ROUND THE LAKE. LOOK, THERE'S ONE RIGHT OPPOSITE.
AND WHAT ARE YOU GOING TO DO?
GET SOME DRY CLOTHES ON AND GO BACK TO THE ORGY. WHAT FUN!
LAKESIDE HOTEL
WHAT'S A FONDUE, ASTERIX?
I EXPECT IT'S SOME KIND OF LOCAL ORGY.
...YES, I HAVE GOT A ROOM FREE, EVEN THOUGH THEY'RE HOLDING THE ICTC – THE INTERNATIONAL CONFERENCE OF TRIBAL CHIEFTAINS – IN GENAVA JUST NOW.
!
THERE WAS A BARBARIAN DELEGATION WHICH DIDN'T WANT THEIR ROOM. THEY SAID IT WAS TOO CLEAN.
YOU MUST BE STRANGERS HERE... I'D BETTER TELL YOU, YOU SHOULD HAVE COME OVER THE BRIDGE. JULIUS CAESAR DESTROYED IT, BUT IT'S BEEN REBUILT NOW.
MEANWHILE, IN THE GOVERNOR'S PALACE...
YOU BUNGLING IDIOTS! I MUST HAVE THOSE GAULS!

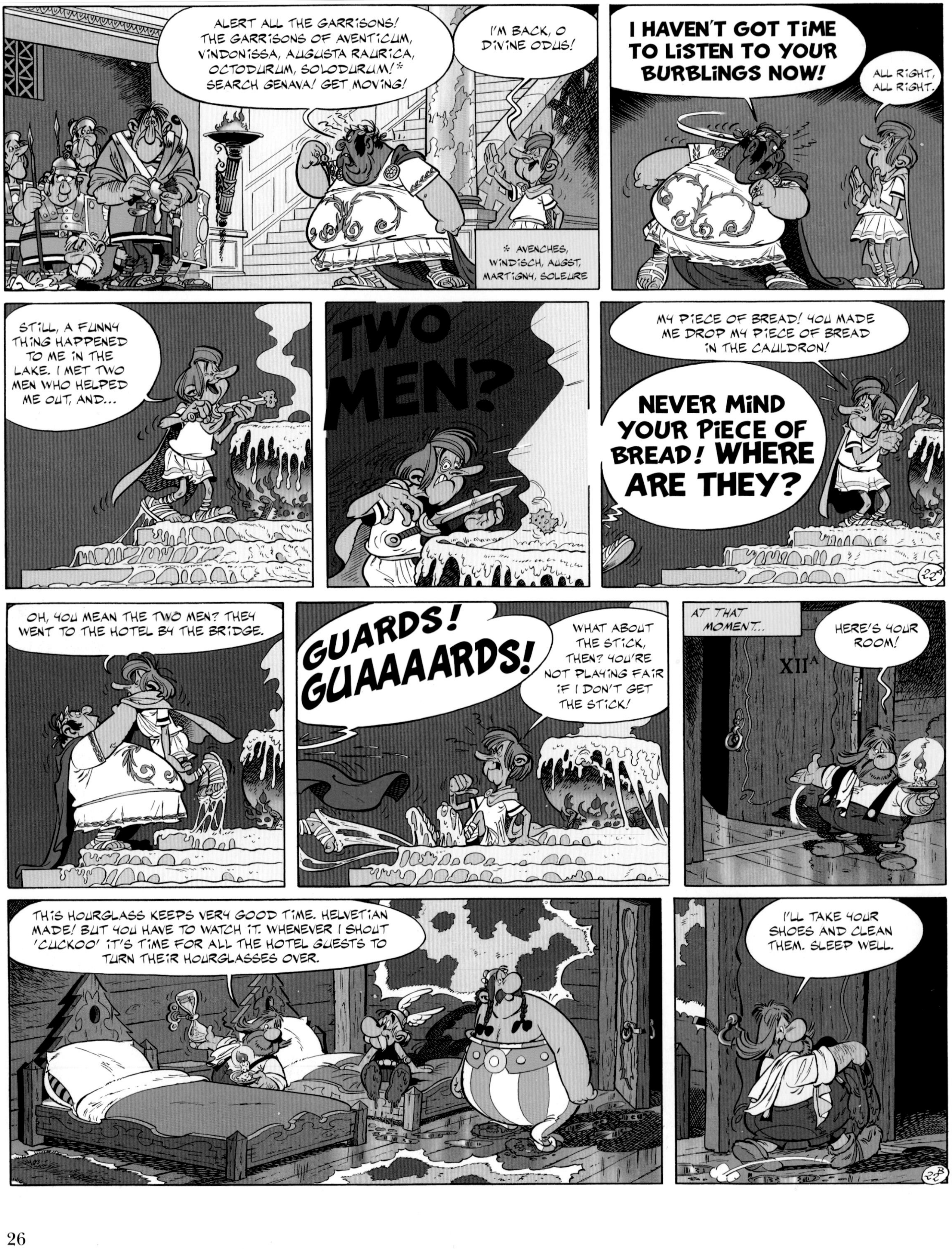
ALERT ALL THE GARRISONS! THE GARRISONS OF AVENTICUM, VINDONISSA, AUGUSTA RAURICA, OCTODURUM, SOLODURUM!* SEARCH GENAVA! GET MOVING!
I'M BACK, O DIVINE ODUS!
* AVENCHES, WINDISCH, AUGST, MARTIGNY, SOLEURE
I HAVEN'T GOT TIME TO LISTEN TO YOUR BURBLINGS NOW!
ALL RIGHT, ALL RIGHT.
STILL, A FUNNY THING HAPPENED TO ME IN THE LAKE. I MET TWO MEN WHO HELPED ME OUT, AND...
TWO MEN?
MY PIECE OF BREAD! YOU MADE ME DROP MY PIECE OF BREAD IN THE CAULDRON!
NEVER MIND YOUR PIECE OF BREAD! WHERE ARE THEY?
OH, YOU MEAN THE TWO MEN? THEY WENT TO THE HOTEL BY THE BRIDGE.
GUARDS! GUAAAARDS!
WHAT ABOUT THE STICK, THEN? YOU'RE NOT PLAYING FAIR IF I DON'T GET THE STICK!
AT THAT MOMENT...
XII^A
HERE'S YOUR ROOM!
THIS HOURGLASS KEEPS VERY GOOD TIME. HELVETIAN MADE! BUT YOU HAVE TO WATCH IT. WHENEVER I SHOUT 'CUCKOO' IT'S TIME FOR ALL THE HOTEL GUESTS TO TURN THEIR HOURGLASSES OVER.
I'LL TAKE YOUR SHOES AND CLEAN THEM. SLEEP WELL.

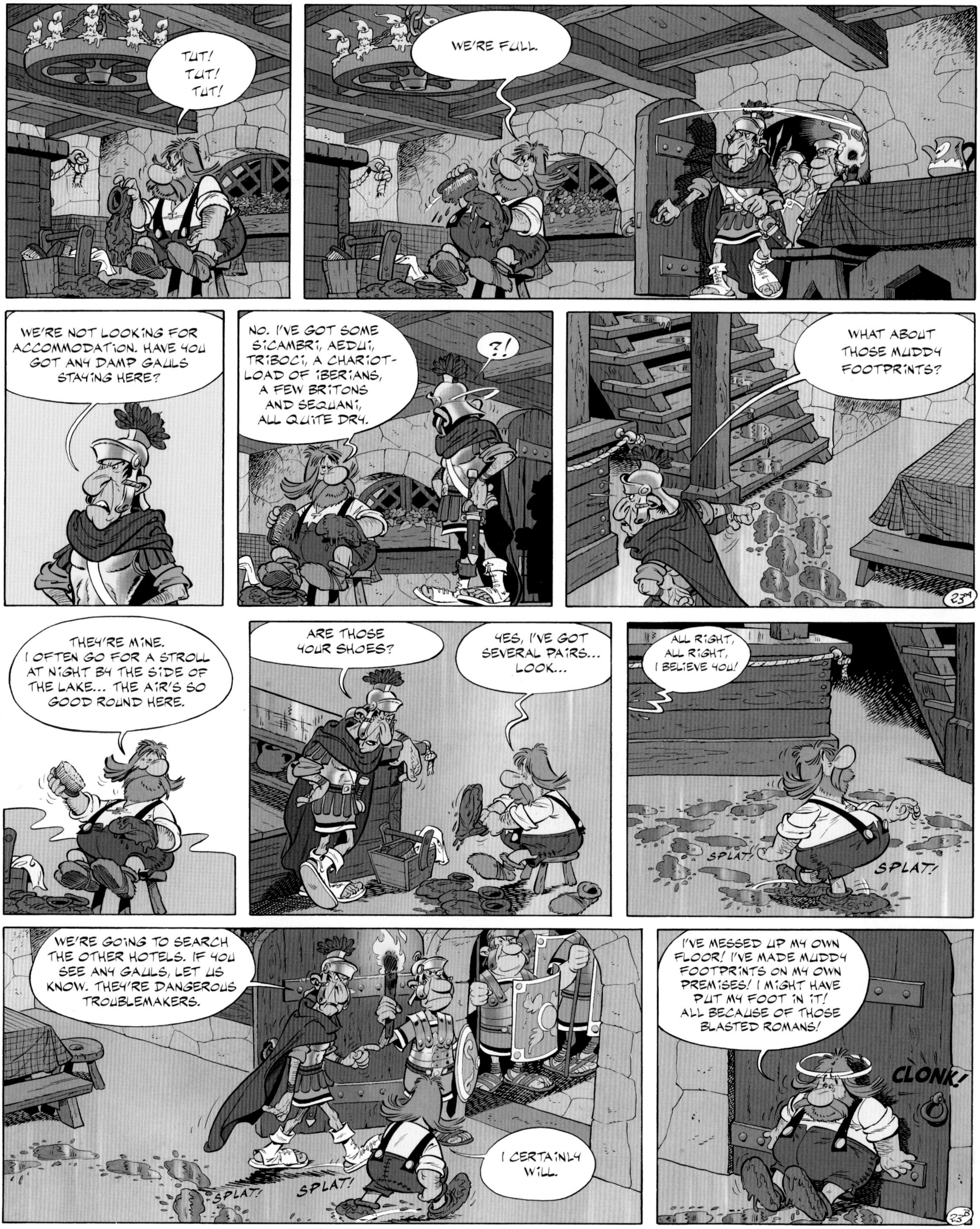
TUT! TUT! TUT!
WE'RE FULL.
WE'RE NOT LOOKING FOR ACCOMMODATION. HAVE YOU GOT ANY DAMP GAULS STAYING HERE?
NO. I'VE GOT SOME SICAMBRI, AEDUI, TRIBOCI, A CHARIOT-LOAD OF IBERIANS, A FEW BRITONS AND SEQUANI, ALL QUITE DRY.
?!
WHAT ABOUT THOSE MUDDY FOOTPRINTS?
THEY'RE MINE. I OFTEN GO FOR A STROLL AT NIGHT BY THE SIDE OF THE LAKE... THE AIR'S SO GOOD ROUND HERE.
ARE THOSE YOUR SHOES?
YES, I'VE GOT SEVERAL PAIRS... LOOK...
ALL RIGHT, ALL RIGHT, I BELIEVE YOU!
SPLAT!
SPLAT!
WE'RE GOING TO SEARCH THE OTHER HOTELS. IF YOU SEE ANY GAULS, LET US KNOW. THEY'RE DANGEROUS TROUBLEMAKERS.
I CERTAINLY WILL.
SPLAT!
SPLAT!
I'VE MESSED UP MY OWN FLOOR! I'VE MADE MUDDY FOOTPRINTS ON MY OWN PREMISES! I MIGHT HAVE PUT MY FOOT IN IT! ALL BECAUSE OF THOSE BLASTED ROMANS!
CLONK!

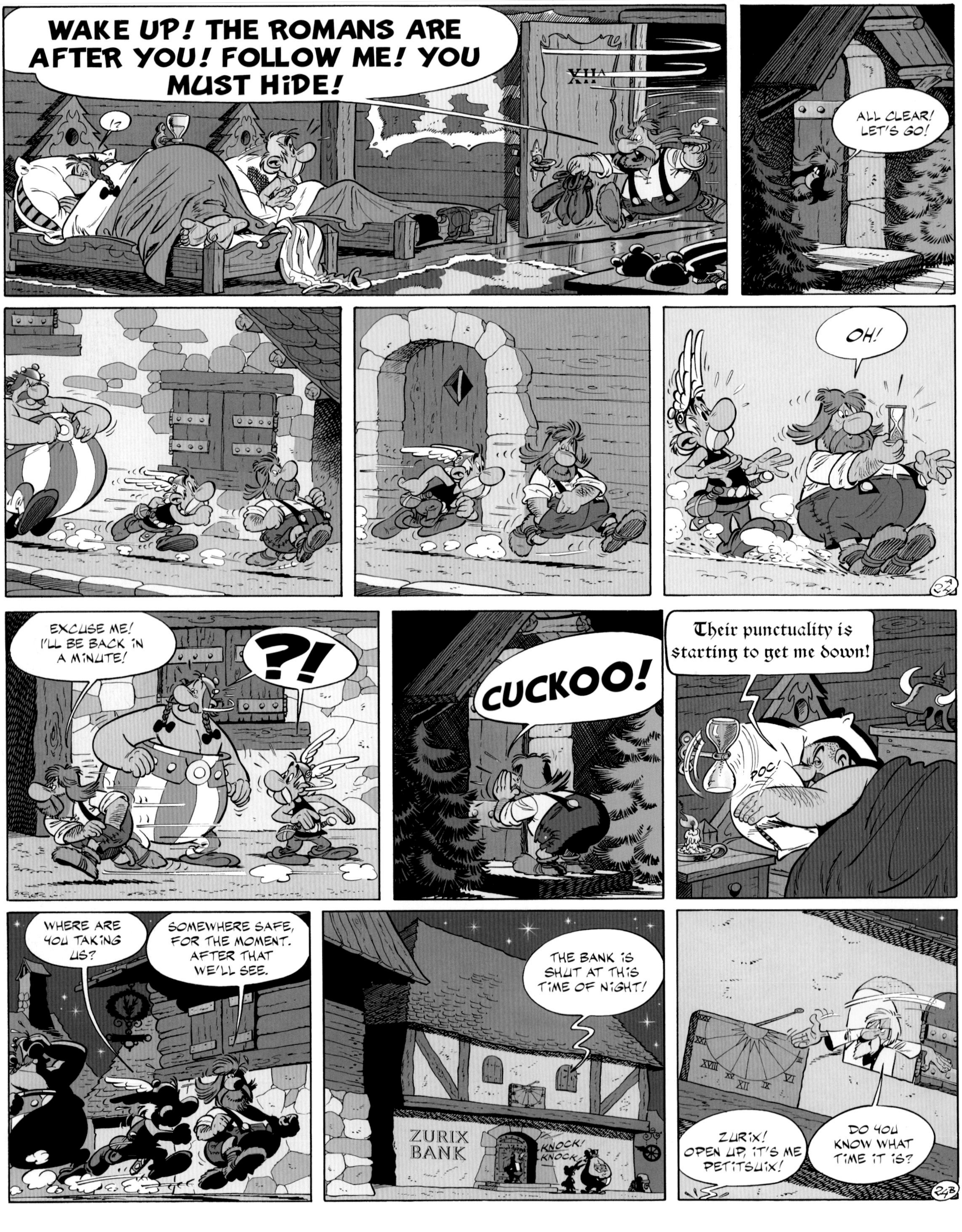
WAKE UP! THE ROMANS ARE AFTER YOU! FOLLOW ME! YOU MUST HIDE!
!?
XII
ALL CLEAR! LET'S GO!
OH!
EXCUSE ME! I'LL BE BACK IN A MINUTE!
?!
CUCKOO!
Their punctuality is starting to get me down!
POC!
WHERE ARE YOU TAKING US?
SOMEWHERE SAFE, FOR THE MOMENT. AFTER THAT WE'LL SEE.
THE BANK IS SHUT AT THIS TIME OF NIGHT!
ZURIX BANK
KNOCK! KNOCK!
ZURIX! OPEN UP, IT'S ME PETITSUIX!
DO YOU KNOW WHAT TIME IT IS?

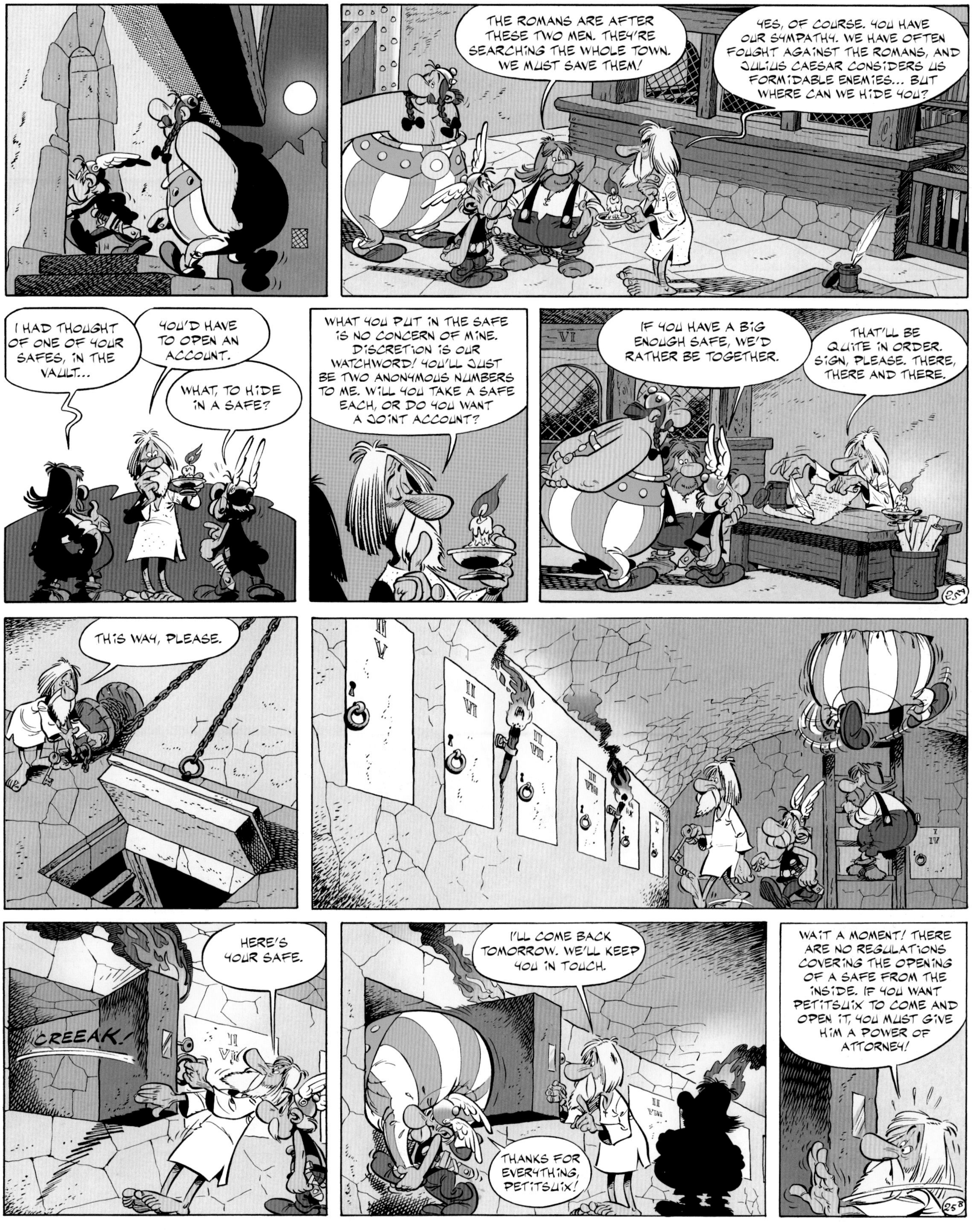
THE ROMANS ARE AFTER THESE TWO MEN. THEY'RE SEARCHING THE WHOLE TOWN. WE MUST SAVE THEM!
YES, OF COURSE. YOU HAVE OUR SYMPATHY. WE HAVE OFTEN FOUGHT AGAINST THE ROMANS, AND JULIUS CAESAR CONSIDERS US FORMIDABLE ENEMIES... BUT WHERE CAN WE HIDE YOU?
I HAD THOUGHT OF ONE OF YOUR SAFES, IN THE VAULT...
YOU'D HAVE TO OPEN AN ACCOUNT.
WHAT, TO HIDE IN A SAFE?
WHAT YOU PUT IN THE SAFE IS NO CONCERN OF MINE. DISCRETION IS OUR WATCHWORD! YOU'LL JUST BE TWO ANONYMOUS NUMBERS TO ME. WILL YOU TAKE A SAFE EACH, OR DO YOU WANT A JOINT ACCOUNT?
IF YOU HAVE A BIG ENOUGH SAFE, WE'D RATHER BE TOGETHER.
THAT'LL BE QUITE IN ORDER. SIGN, PLEASE. THERE, THERE AND THERE.
THIS WAY, PLEASE.
HERE'S YOUR SAFE.
CREEAK!
I'LL COME BACK TOMORROW. WE'LL KEEP YOU IN TOUCH.
THANKS FOR EVERYTHING, PETITSUIX!
WAIT A MOMENT! THERE ARE NO REGULATIONS COVERING THE OPENING OF A SAFE FROM THE INSIDE. IF YOU WANT PETITSUIX TO COME AND OPEN IT, YOU MUST GIVE HIM A POWER OF ATTORNEY!

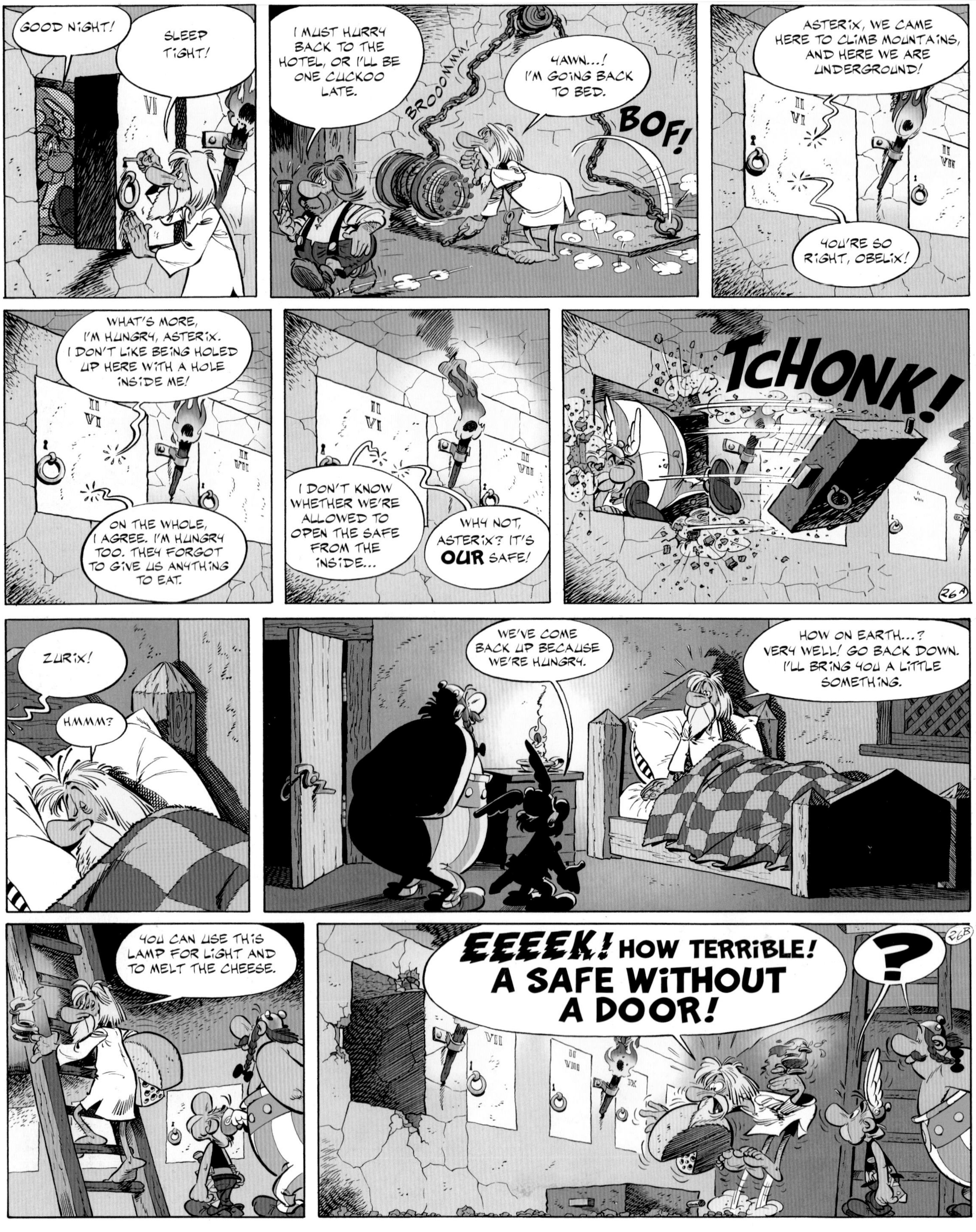
GOOD NIGHT!
SLEEP TIGHT!
I MUST HURRY BACK TO THE HOTEL, OR I'LL BE ONE CUCKOO LATE.
BROOOMM!
YAWN...! I'M GOING BACK TO BED.
BOF!
ASTERIX, WE CAME HERE TO CLIMB MOUNTAINS, AND HERE WE ARE UNDERGROUND!
YOU'RE SO RIGHT, OBELIX!
WHAT'S MORE, I'M HUNGRY, ASTERIX. I DON'T LIKE BEING HOLED UP HERE WITH A HOLE INSIDE ME!
ON THE WHOLE, I AGREE. I'M HUNGRY TOO. THEY FORGOT TO GIVE US ANYTHING TO EAT.
I DON'T KNOW WHETHER WE'RE ALLOWED TO OPEN THE SAFE FROM THE INSIDE...
WHY NOT, ASTERIX? IT'S OUR SAFE!
TCHONK!
ZURIX!
HMMM?
WE'VE COME BACK UP BECAUSE WE'RE HUNGRY.
HOW ON EARTH...? VERY WELL! GO BACK DOWN. I'LL BRING YOU A LITTLE SOMETHING.
YOU CAN USE THIS LAMP FOR LIGHT AND TO MELT THE CHEESE.
EEEEK! HOW TERRIBLE! A SAFE WITHOUT A DOOR!
?

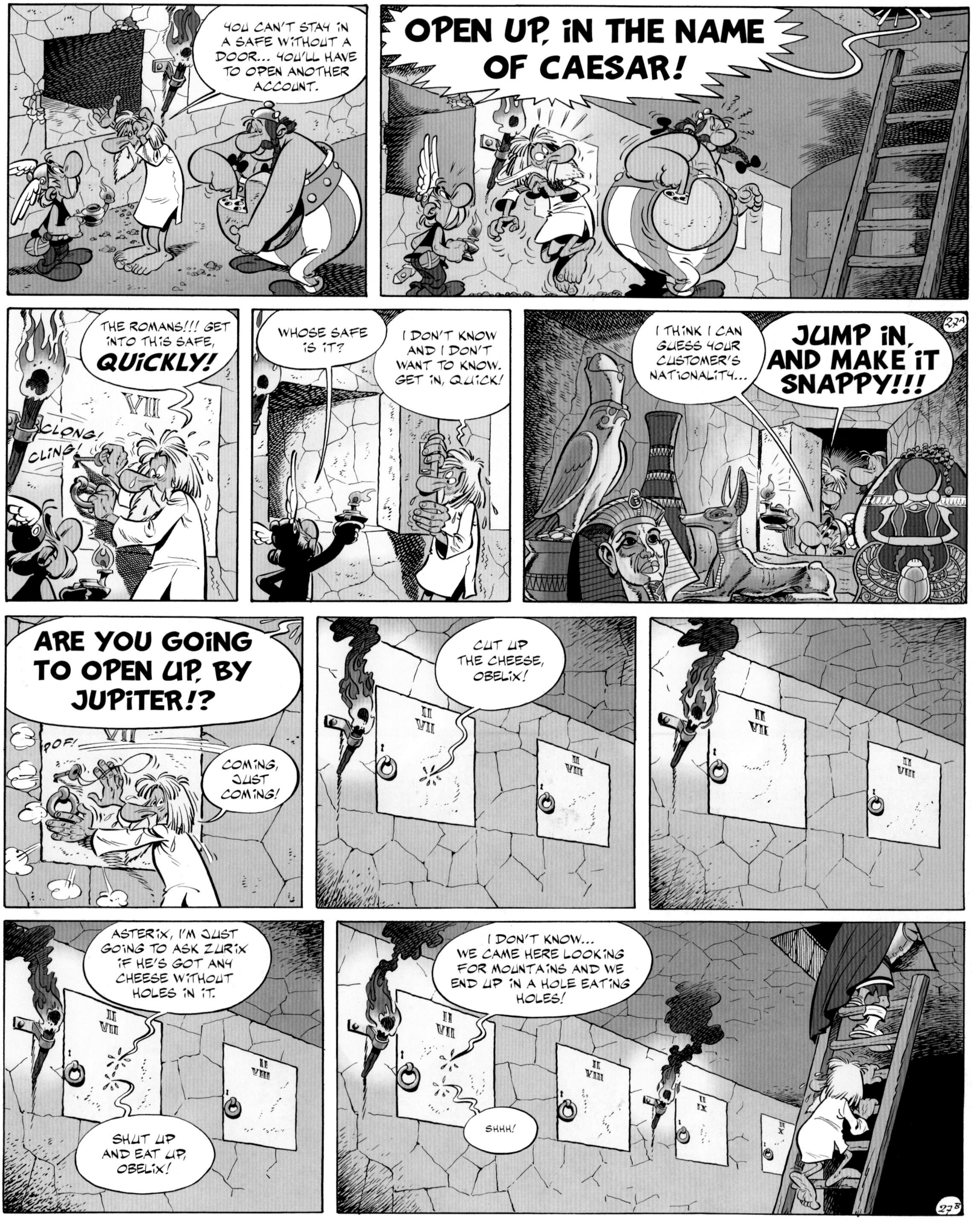

YOU CAN'T STAY IN A SAFE WITHOUT A DOOR... YOU'LL HAVE TO OPEN ANOTHER ACCOUNT.
OPEN UP, IN THE NAME OF CAESAR!
THE ROMANS!!! GET INTO THIS SAFE, QUICKLY!
VII
CLONG!
CLING!
WHOSE SAFE IS IT?
I DON'T KNOW AND I DON'T WANT TO KNOW. GET IN, QUICK!
I THINK I CAN GUESS YOUR CUSTOMER'S NATIONALITY...
JUMP IN, AND MAKE IT SNAPPY!!!
ARE YOU GOING TO OPEN UP, BY JUPITER!?
POF!
COMING, JUST COMING!
CUT UP THE CHEESE, OBELIX!
ASTERIX, I'M JUST GOING TO ASK ZURIX IF HE'S GOT ANY CHEESE WITHOUT HOLES IN IT.
SHUT UP AND EAT UP, OBELIX!
I DON'T KNOW... WE CAME HERE LOOKING FOR MOUNTAINS AND WE END UP IN A HOLE EATING HOLES!
SHHH!

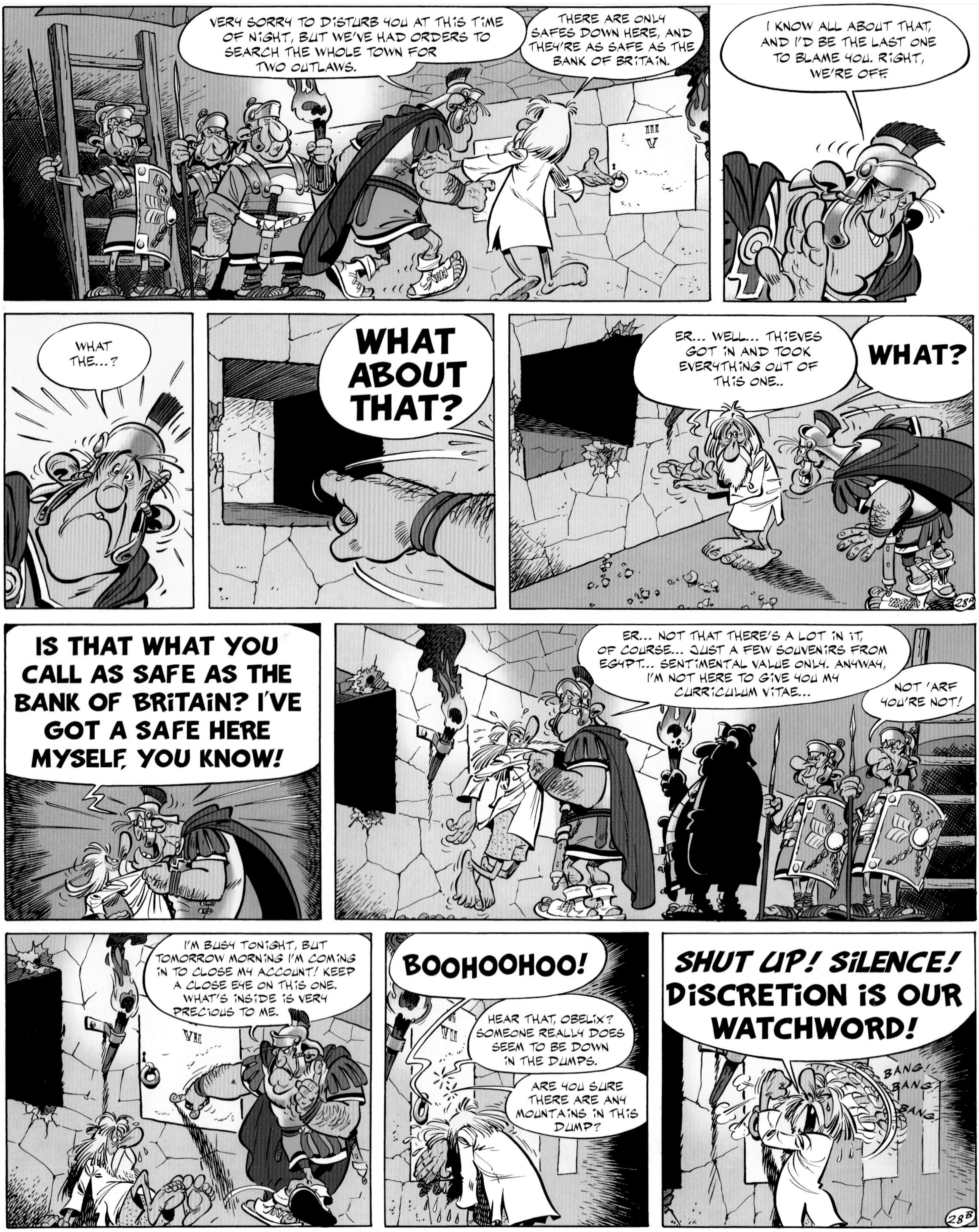
VERY SORRY TO DISTURB YOU AT THIS TIME OF NIGHT, BUT WE'VE HAD ORDERS TO SEARCH THE WHOLE TOWN FOR TWO OUTLAWS.
THERE ARE ONLY SAFES DOWN HERE, AND THEY'RE AS SAFE AS THE BANK OF BRITAIN.
I KNOW ALL ABOUT THAT, AND I'D BE THE LAST ONE TO BLAME YOU. RIGHT, WE'RE OFF.
WHAT THE...?
WHAT ABOUT THAT?
ER... WELL... THIEVES GOT IN AND TOOK EVERYTHING OUT OF THIS ONE..
WHAT?
IS THAT WHAT YOU CALL AS SAFE AS THE BANK OF BRITAIN? I'VE GOT A SAFE HERE MYSELF, YOU KNOW!
ER... NOT THAT THERE'S A LOT IN IT, OF COURSE... JUST A FEW SOUVENIRS FROM EGYPT... SENTIMENTAL VALUE ONLY. ANYWAY, I'M NOT HERE TO GIVE YOU MY CURRICULUM VITAE...
NOT 'ARF YOU'RE NOT!
I'M BUSY TONIGHT, BUT TOMORROW MORNING I'M COMING IN TO CLOSE MY ACCOUNT! KEEP A CLOSE EYE ON THIS ONE. WHAT'S INSIDE IS VERY PRECIOUS TO ME.
BOOHOOHOO!
HEAR THAT, OBELIX? SOMEONE REALLY DOES SEEM TO BE DOWN IN THE DUMPS.
ARE YOU SURE THERE ARE ANY MOUNTAINS IN THIS DUMP?
SHUT UP! SILENCE! DISCRETION IS OUR WATCHWORD!
BANG
BANG
BANG

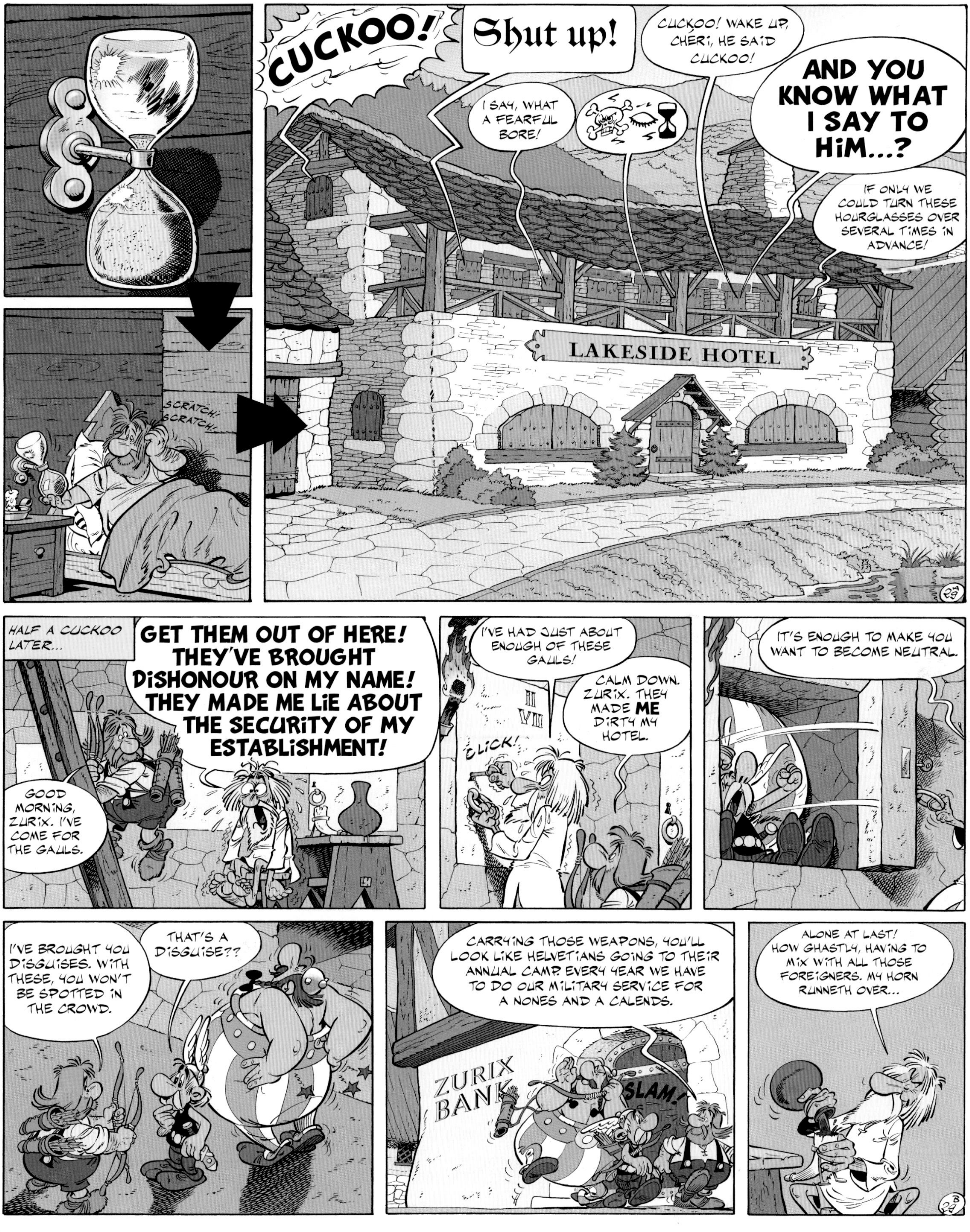

CUCKOO!
Shut up!
CUCKOO! WAKE UP, CHERI, HE SAID CUCKOO!
AND YOU KNOW WHAT I SAY TO HIM...?
I SAY, WHAT A FEARFUL BORE!
IF ONLY WE COULD TURN THESE HOURGLASSES OVER SEVERAL TIMES IN ADVANCE!
LAKESIDE HOTEL
SCRATCH! SCRATCH!
HALF A CUCKOO LATER...
GET THEM OUT OF HERE! THEY'VE BROUGHT DISHONOUR ON MY NAME! THEY MADE ME LIE ABOUT THE SECURITY OF MY ESTABLISHMENT!
GOOD MORNING, ZURIX. I'VE COME FOR THE GAULS.
I'VE HAD JUST ABOUT ENOUGH OF THESE GAULS!
CALM DOWN, ZURIX. THEY MADE ME DIRTY MY HOTEL.
CLICK!
IT'S ENOUGH TO MAKE YOU WANT TO BECOME NEUTRAL.
I'VE BROUGHT YOU DISGUISES. WITH THESE, YOU WON'T BE SPOTTED IN THE CROWD.
THAT'S A DISGUISE??
CARRYING THOSE WEAPONS, YOU'LL LOOK LIKE HELVETIANS GOING TO THEIR ANNUAL CAMP. EVERY YEAR WE HAVE TO DO OUR MILITARY SERVICE FOR A NONES AND A CALENDS.
ZURIX BANK
SLAM!
ALONE AT LAST! HOW GHASTLY, HAVING TO MIX WITH ALL THOSE FOREIGNERS. MY HORN RUNNETH OVER...

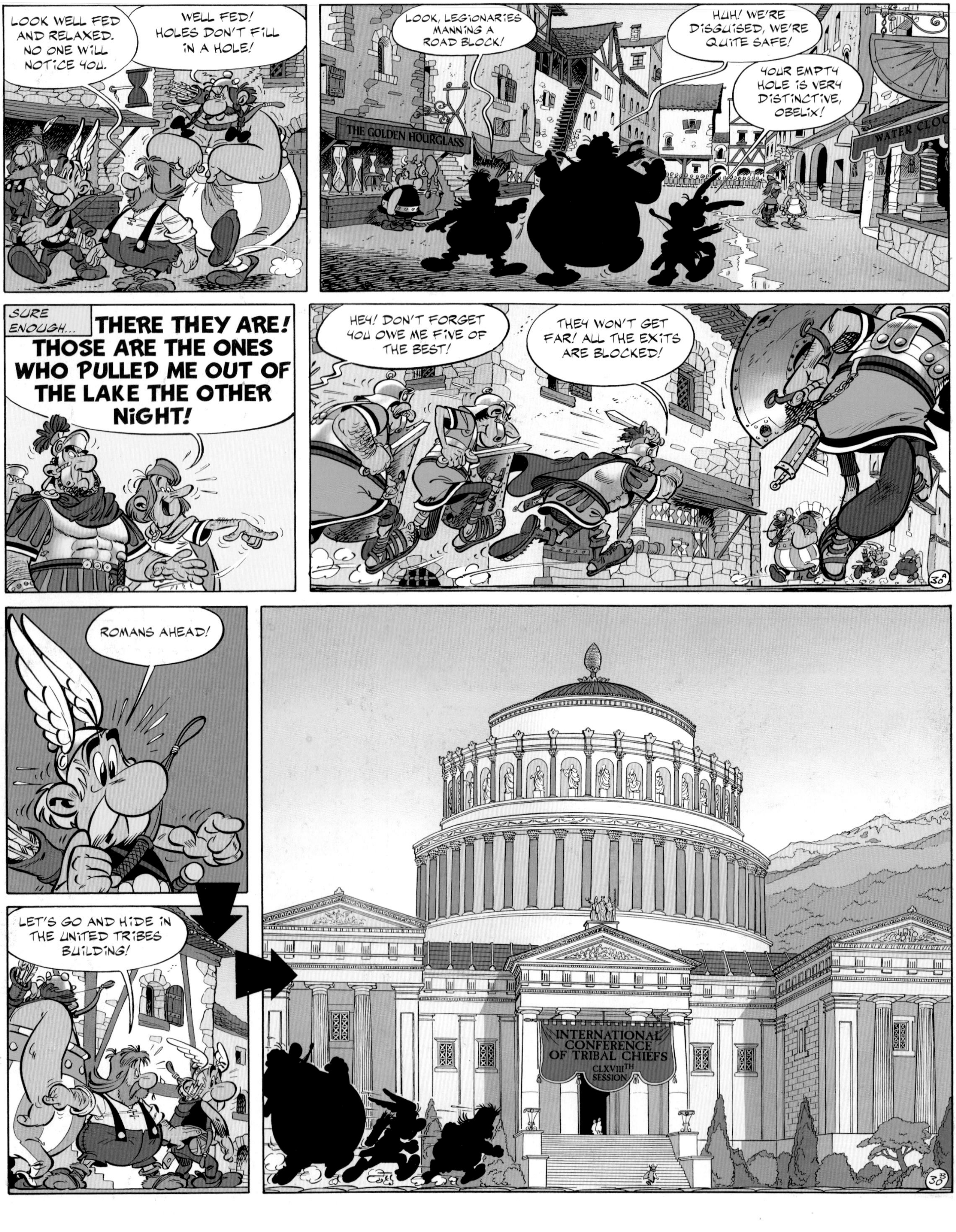
LOOK WELL FED AND RELAXED. NO ONE WILL NOTICE YOU.
WELL FED! HOLES DON'T FILL IN A HOLE!
LOOK, LEGIONARIES MANNING A ROAD BLOCK!
THE GOLDEN HOURGLASS
HUH! WE'RE DISGUISED, WE'RE QUITE SAFE!
YOUR EMPTY HOLE IS VERY DISTINCTIVE, OBELIX!
WATER CLOC
SURE ENOUGH...
THERE THEY ARE! THOSE ARE THE ONES WHO PULLED ME OUT OF THE LAKE THE OTHER NIGHT!
HEY! DON'T FORGET YOU OWE ME FIVE OF THE BEST!
THEY WON'T GET FAR! ALL THE EXITS ARE BLOCKED!
ROMANS AHEAD!
LET'S GO AND HIDE IN THE UNITED TRIBES BUILDING!
INTERNATIONAL CONFERENCE OF TRIBAL CHIEFS CLXVIIITH SESSION

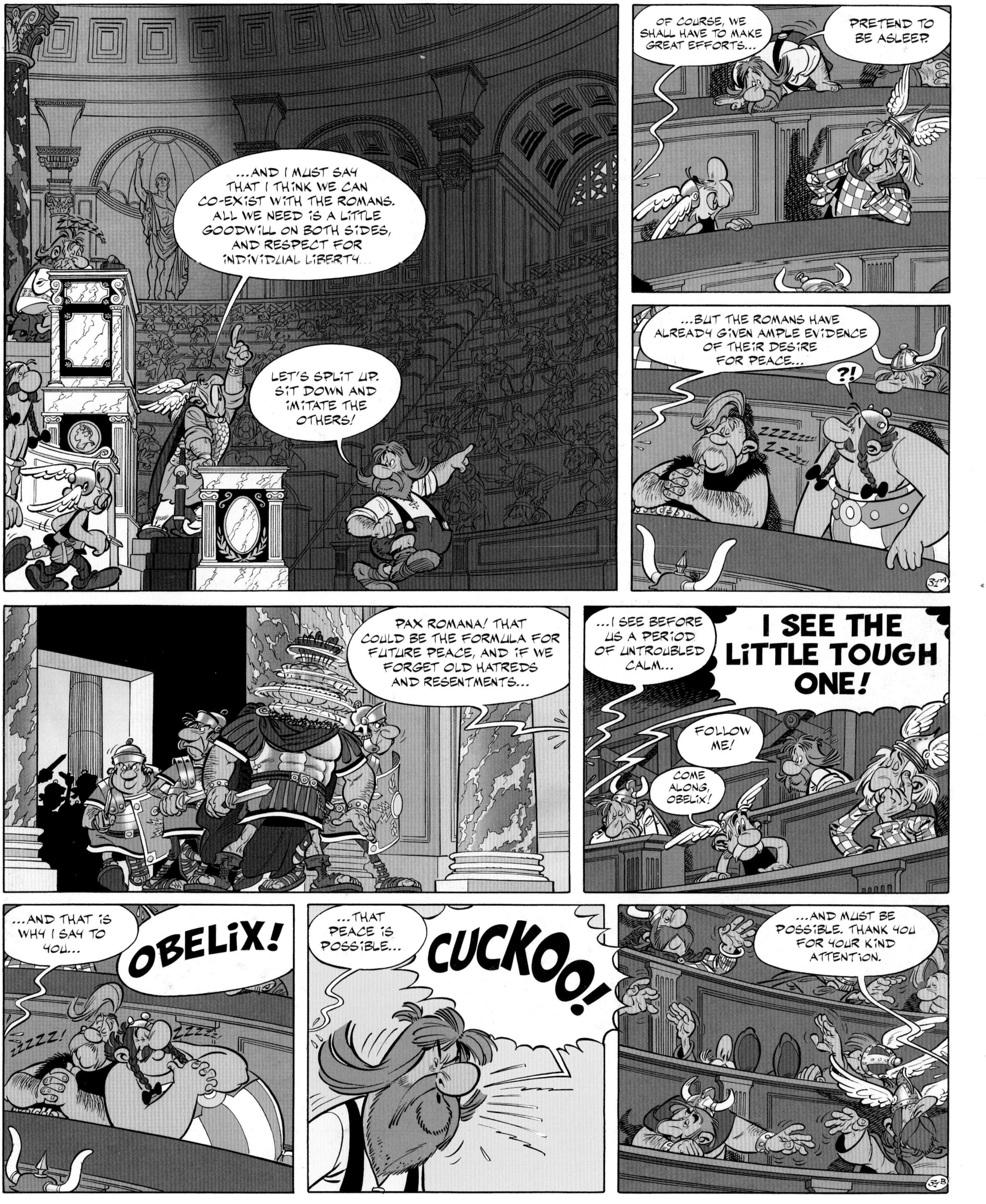

...AND I MUST SAY THAT I THINK WE CAN CO-EXIST WITH THE ROMANS. ALL WE NEED IS A LITTLE GOODWILL ON BOTH SIDES, AND RESPECT FOR INDIVIDUAL LIBERTY...
LET'S SPLIT UP. SIT DOWN AND IMITATE THE OTHERS!
OF COURSE, WE SHALL HAVE TO MAKE GREAT EFFORTS...
PRETEND TO BE ASLEEP?
...BUT THE ROMANS HAVE ALREADY GIVEN AMPLE EVIDENCE OF THEIR DESIRE FOR PEACE...
?!
ZZZZZZZ
ZZZZZ
PAX ROMANA! THAT COULD BE THE FORMULA FOR FUTURE PEACE, AND IF WE FORGET OLD HATREDS AND RESENTMENTS...
...I SEE BEFORE US A PERIOD OF UNTROUBLED CALM...
I SEE THE LITTLE TOUGH ONE!
FOLLOW ME!
COME ALONG, OBELIX!
...AND THAT IS WHY I SAY TO YOU...
OBELIX!
ZZZZ!
ZZZZ
...THAT PEACE IS POSSIBLE...
CUCKOO!
...AND MUST BE POSSIBLE. THANK YOU FOR YOUR KIND ATTENTION.

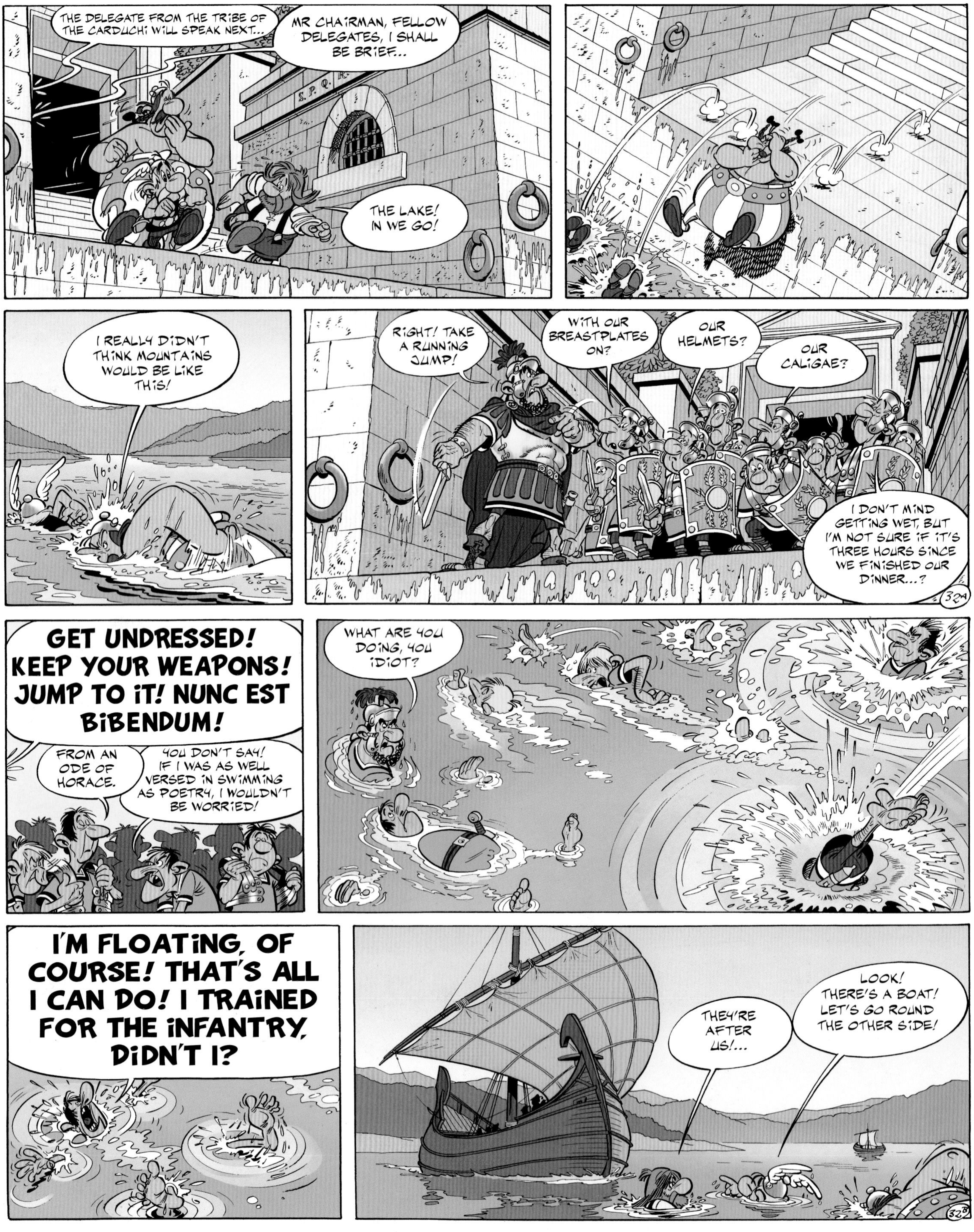
THE DELEGATE FROM THE TRIBE OF THE CARDUCHI WILL SPEAK NEXT...
MR CHAIRMAN, FELLOW DELEGATES, I SHALL BE BRIEF...
S.P.Q.R.
THE LAKE! IN WE GO!
I REALLY DIDN'T THINK MOUNTAINS WOULD BE LIKE THIS!
RIGHT! TAKE A RUNNING JUMP!
WITH OUR BREASTPLATES ON?
OUR HELMETS?
OUR CALIGAE?
I DON'T MIND GETTING WET, BUT I'M NOT SURE IF IT'S THREE HOURS SINCE WE FINISHED OUR DINNER...?
GET UNDRESSED! KEEP YOUR WEAPONS! JUMP TO IT! NUNC EST BIBENDUM!
FROM AN ODE OF HORACE.
YOU DON'T SAY! IF I WAS AS WELL VERSED IN SWIMMING AS POETRY, I WOULDN'T BE WORRIED!
WHAT ARE YOU DOING, YOU IDIOT?
I'M FLOATING, OF COURSE! THAT'S ALL I CAN DO! I TRAINED FOR THE INFANTRY, DIDN'T I?
THEY'RE AFTER US!...
LOOK! THERE'S A BOAT! LET'S GO ROUND THE OTHER SIDE!

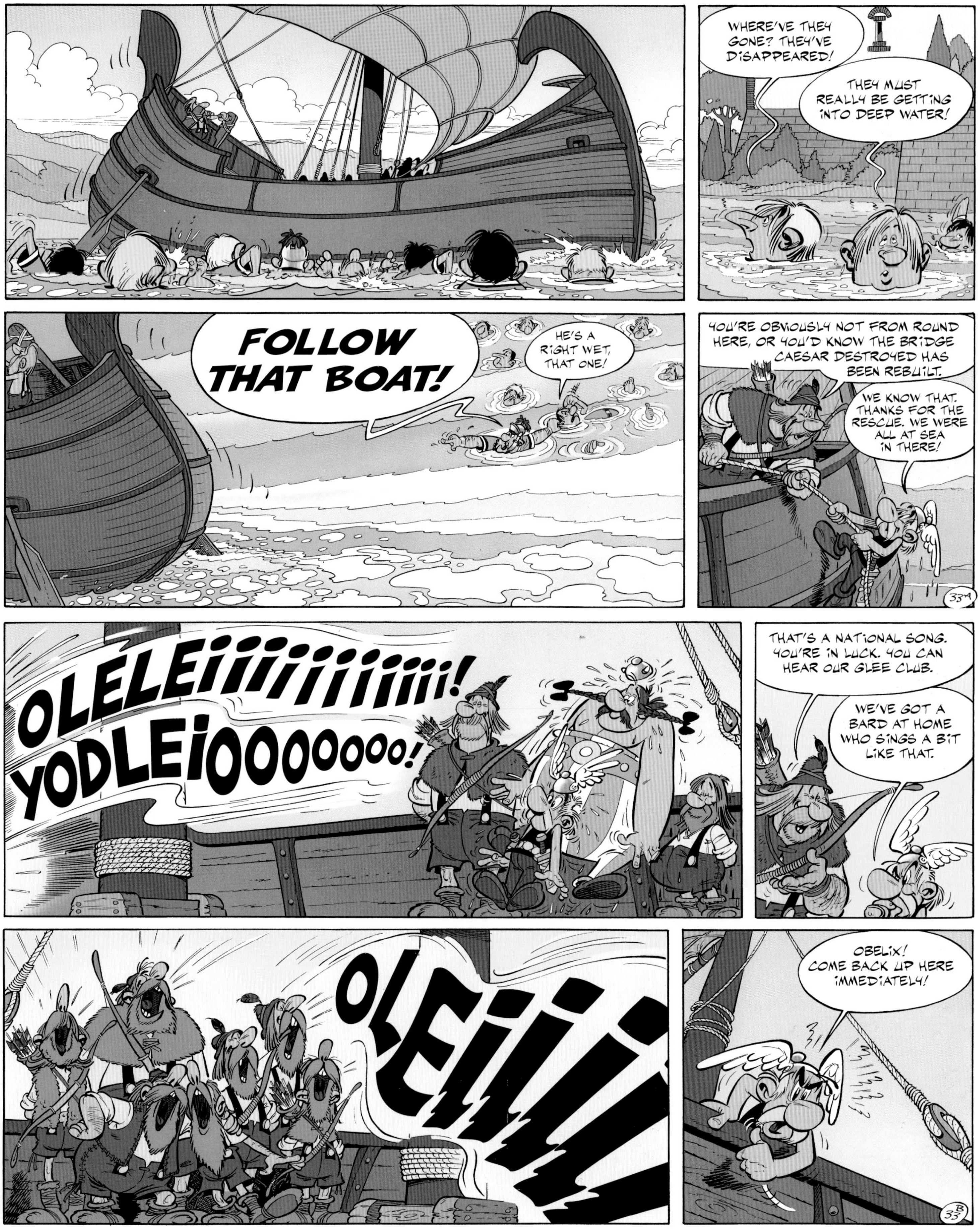

WHERE'VE THEY GONE? THEY'VE DISAPPEARED!
THEY MUST REALLY BE GETTING INTO DEEP WATER!
FOLLOW THAT BOAT!
HE'S A RIGHT WET, THAT ONE!
YOU'RE OBVIOUSLY NOT FROM ROUND HERE, OR YOU'D KNOW THE BRIDGE CAESAR DESTROYED HAS BEEN REBUILT.
WE KNOW THAT. THANKS FOR THE RESCUE. WE WERE ALL AT SEA IN THERE!
OLELEiiiiiiiiii!
YODLEIOOOOOOO!
THAT'S A NATIONAL SONG. YOU'RE IN LUCK. YOU CAN HEAR OUR GLEE CLUB.
WE'VE GOT A BARD AT HOME WHO SINGS A BIT LIKE THAT.
OLEiiii
OBELIX! COME BACK UP HERE IMMEDIATELY!

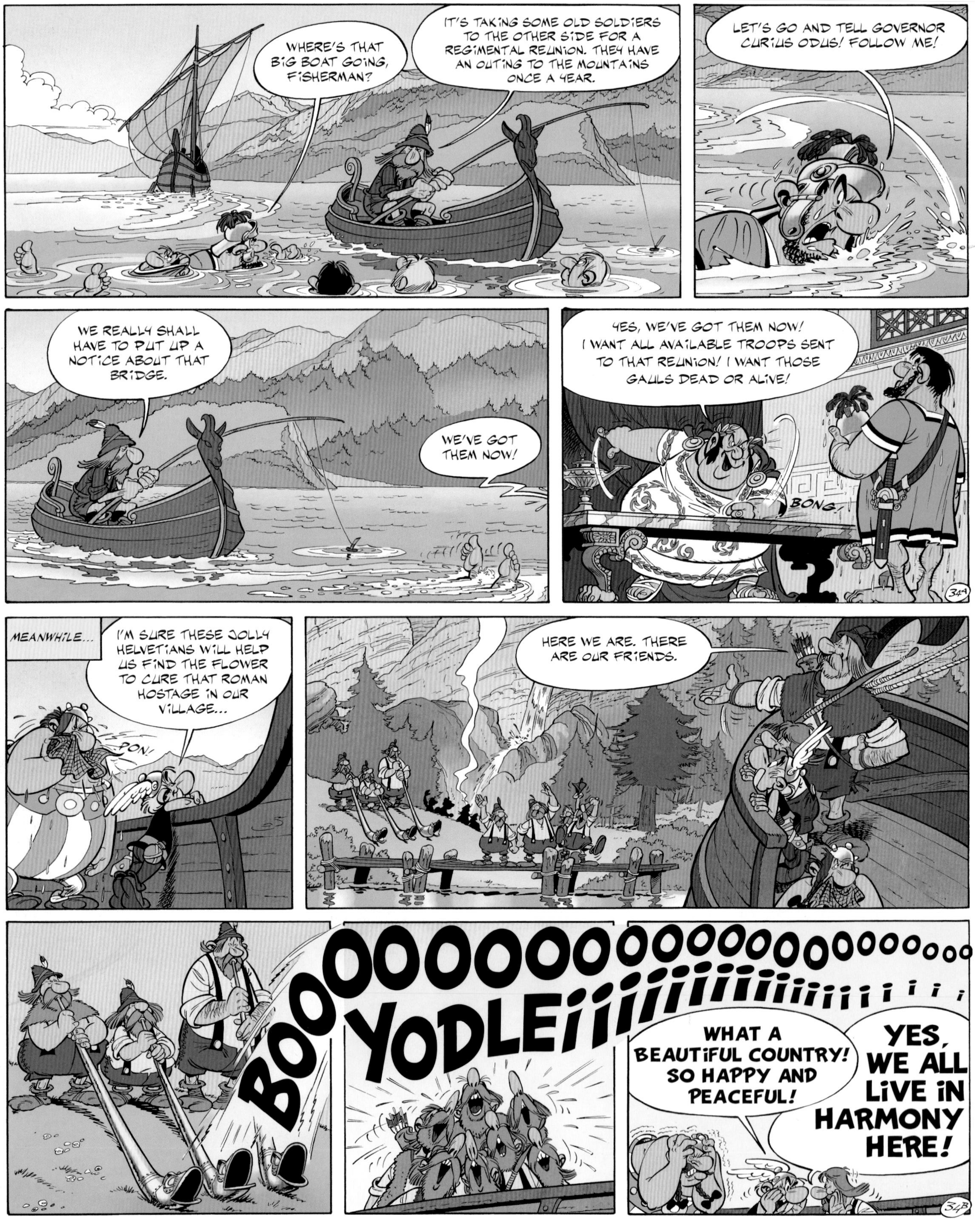
WHERE'S THAT BIG BOAT GOING, FISHERMAN?
IT'S TAKING SOME OLD SOLDIERS TO THE OTHER SIDE FOR A REGIMENTAL REUNION. THEY HAVE AN OUTING TO THE MOUNTAINS ONCE A YEAR.
LET'S GO AND TELL GOVERNOR CURIUS ODUS! FOLLOW ME!
WE REALLY SHALL HAVE TO PUT UP A NOTICE ABOUT THAT BRIDGE.
WE'VE GOT THEM NOW!
YES, WE'VE GOT THEM NOW! I WANT ALL AVAILABLE TROOPS SENT TO THAT REUNION! I WANT THOSE GAULS DEAD OR ALIVE!
BONG
MEANWHILE...
I'M SURE THESE JOLLY HELVETIANS WILL HELP US FIND THE FLOWER TO CURE THAT ROMAN HOSTAGE IN OUR VILLAGE...
PON!
HERE WE ARE. THERE ARE OUR FRIENDS.
BOOOOOOOOOOOOOOOOOOOOOOooo
YODLEiiiiiiiiiiiiiiiiiiii
WHAT A BEAUTIFUL COUNTRY! SO HAPPY AND PEACEFUL!
YES, WE ALL LIVE IN HARMONY HERE!

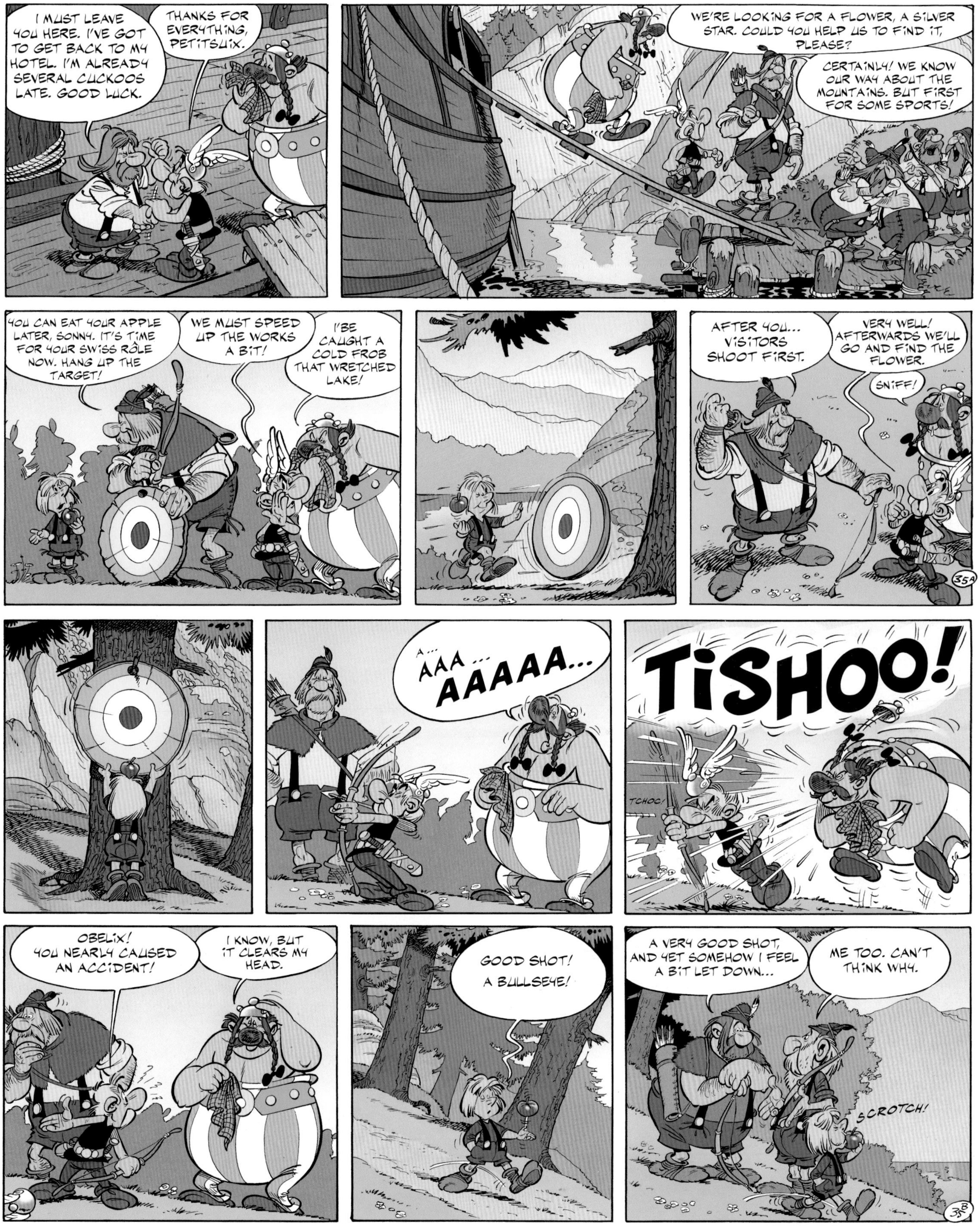
I MUST LEAVE YOU HERE. I'VE GOT TO GET BACK TO MY HOTEL. I'M ALREADY SEVERAL CUCKOOS LATE. GOOD LUCK.
THANKS FOR EVERYTHING, PETITSUIX.
WE'RE LOOKING FOR A FLOWER, A SILVER STAR. COULD YOU HELP US TO FIND IT, PLEASE?
CERTAINLY! WE KNOW OUR WAY ABOUT THE MOUNTAINS. BUT FIRST FOR SOME SPORTS!
YOU CAN EAT YOUR APPLE LATER, SONNY. IT'S TIME FOR YOUR SWISS RÔLE NOW. HANG UP THE TARGET!
WE MUST SPEED UP THE WORKS A BIT!
I'BE CAUGHT A COLD FROB THAT WRETCHED LAKE!
AFTER YOU... VISITORS SHOOT FIRST.
VERY WELL! AFTERWARDS WE'LL GO AND FIND THE FLOWER.
SNIFF!
A... AAA... AAAAA...
TISHOO!
TCHOO!
OBELIX! YOU NEARLY CAUSED AN ACCIDENT!
I KNOW, BUT IT CLEARS MY HEAD.
GOOD SHOT! A BULLSEYE!
A VERY GOOD SHOT, AND YET SOMEHOW I FEEL A BIT LET DOWN...
ME TOO. CAN'T THINK WHY.
SCROTCH!

41

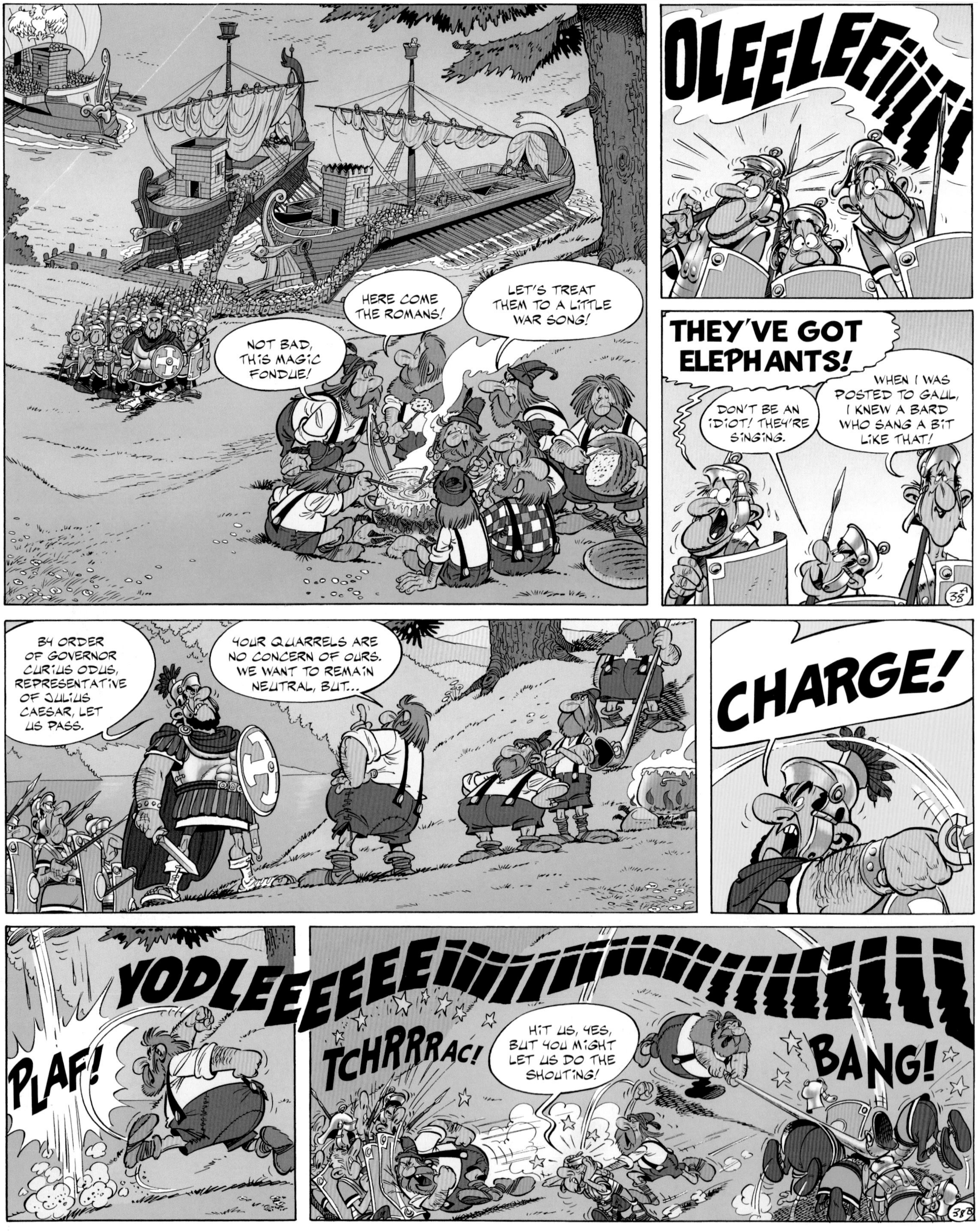
HERE COME THE ROMANS!
LET'S TREAT THEM TO A LITTLE WAR SONG!
NOT BAD, THIS MAGIC FONDUE!
OLEELEEiiiiii
THEY'VE GOT ELEPHANTS!
DON'T BE AN iDIOT! THEY'RE SiNGiNG.
WHEN I WAS POSTED TO GAUL, I KNEW A BARD WHO SANG A BIT LIKE THAT!
BY ORDER OF GOVERNOR CURIUS ODUS, REPRESENTATIVE OF JULIUS CAESAR, LET US PASS.
YOUR QUARRELS ARE NO CONCERN OF OURS. WE WANT TO REMAIN NEUTRAL, BUT...
CHARGE!
YODLEEEEEEiiiiiiiiiiiiiiiiiiii
PLAF!
TCHRRRAC!
HiT US, YES, BUT YOU MiGHT LET US DO THE SHOUTiNG!
BANG!

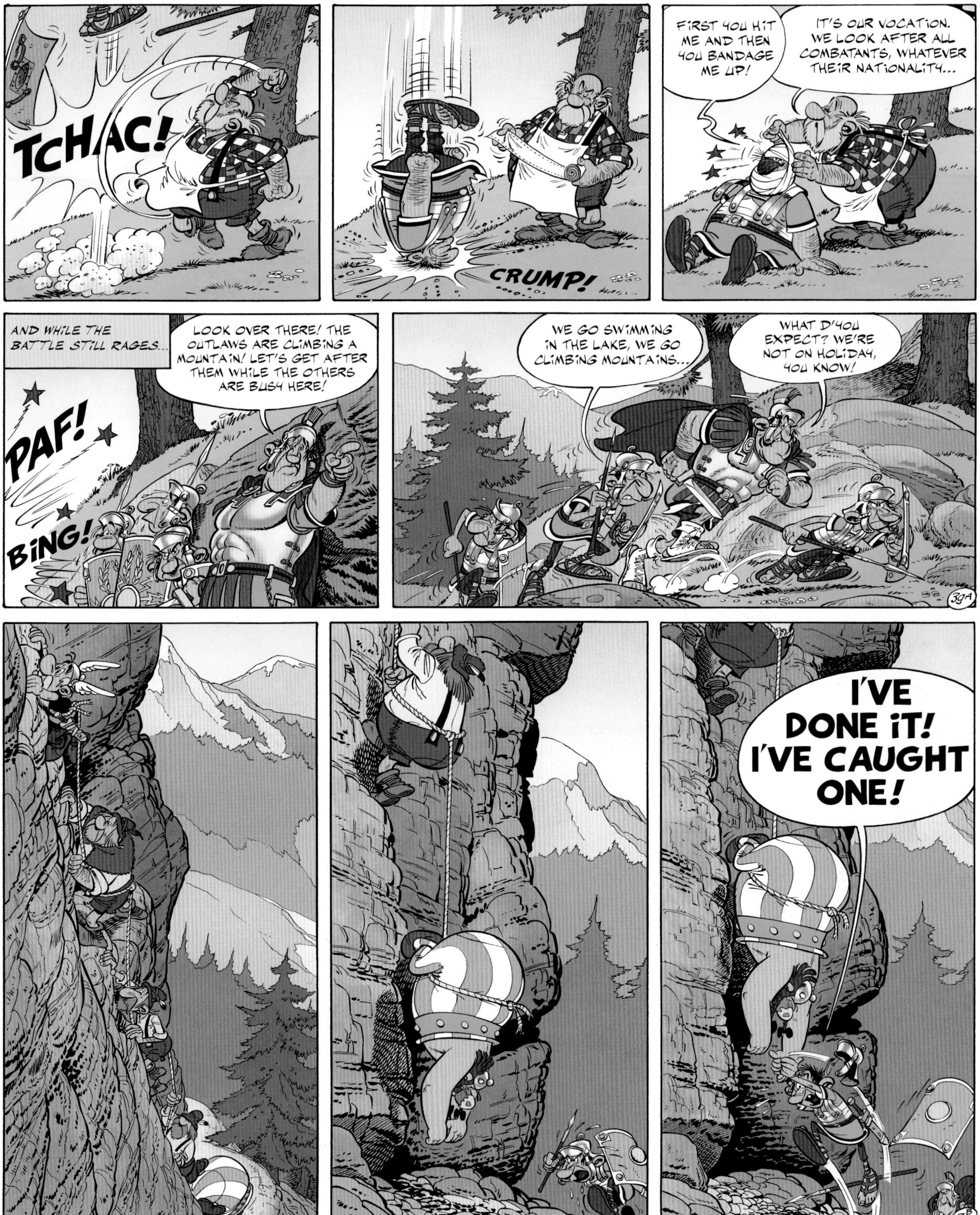

TCHAC!
CRUMP!
FIRST YOU HIT ME AND THEN YOU BANDAGE ME UP!
IT'S OUR VOCATION. WE LOOK AFTER ALL COMBATANTS, WHATEVER THEIR NATIONALITY...
AND WHILE THE BATTLE STILL RAGES...
LOOK OVER THERE! THE OUTLAWS ARE CLIMBING A MOUNTAIN! LET'S GET AFTER THEM WHILE THE OTHERS ARE BUSY HERE!
PAF!
BING!
WE GO SWIMMING IN THE LAKE, WE GO CLIMBING MOUNTAINS...
WHAT D'YOU EXPECT? WE'RE NOT ON HOLIDAY, YOU KNOW!
39A
I'VE DONE IT! I'VE CAUGHT ONE!
39B

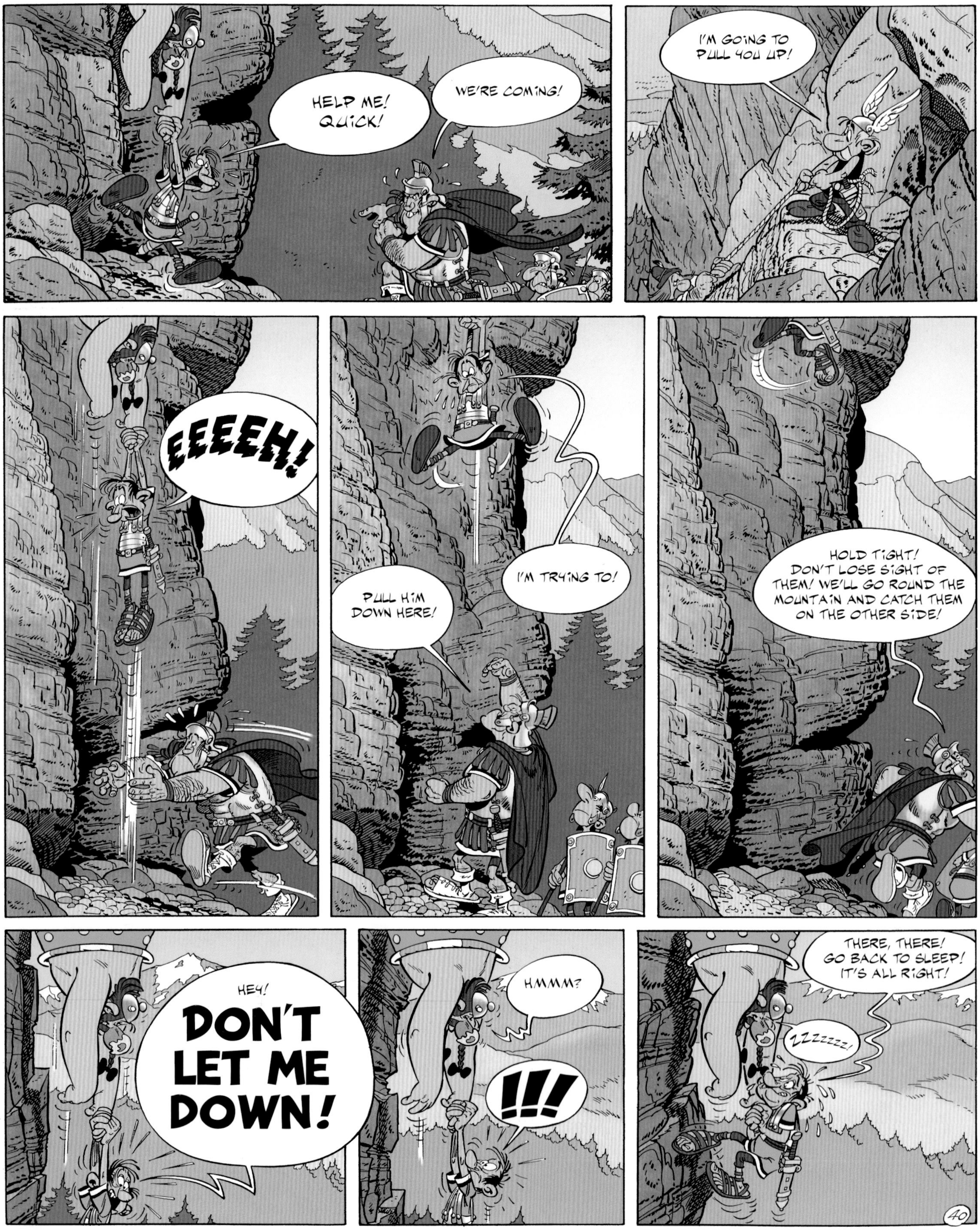

HELP ME! QUICK!
WE'RE COMING!
I'M GOING TO PULL YOU UP!
EEEEH!
I'M TRYING TO!
PULL HIM DOWN HERE!
HOLD TIGHT! DON'T LOSE SIGHT OF THEM! WE'LL GO ROUND THE MOUNTAIN AND CATCH THEM ON THE OTHER SIDE!
HEY!
DON'T LET ME DOWN!
HMMM?
!!!
THERE, THERE! GO BACK TO SLEEP! IT'S ALL RIGHT!
ZZZzzzz!
40

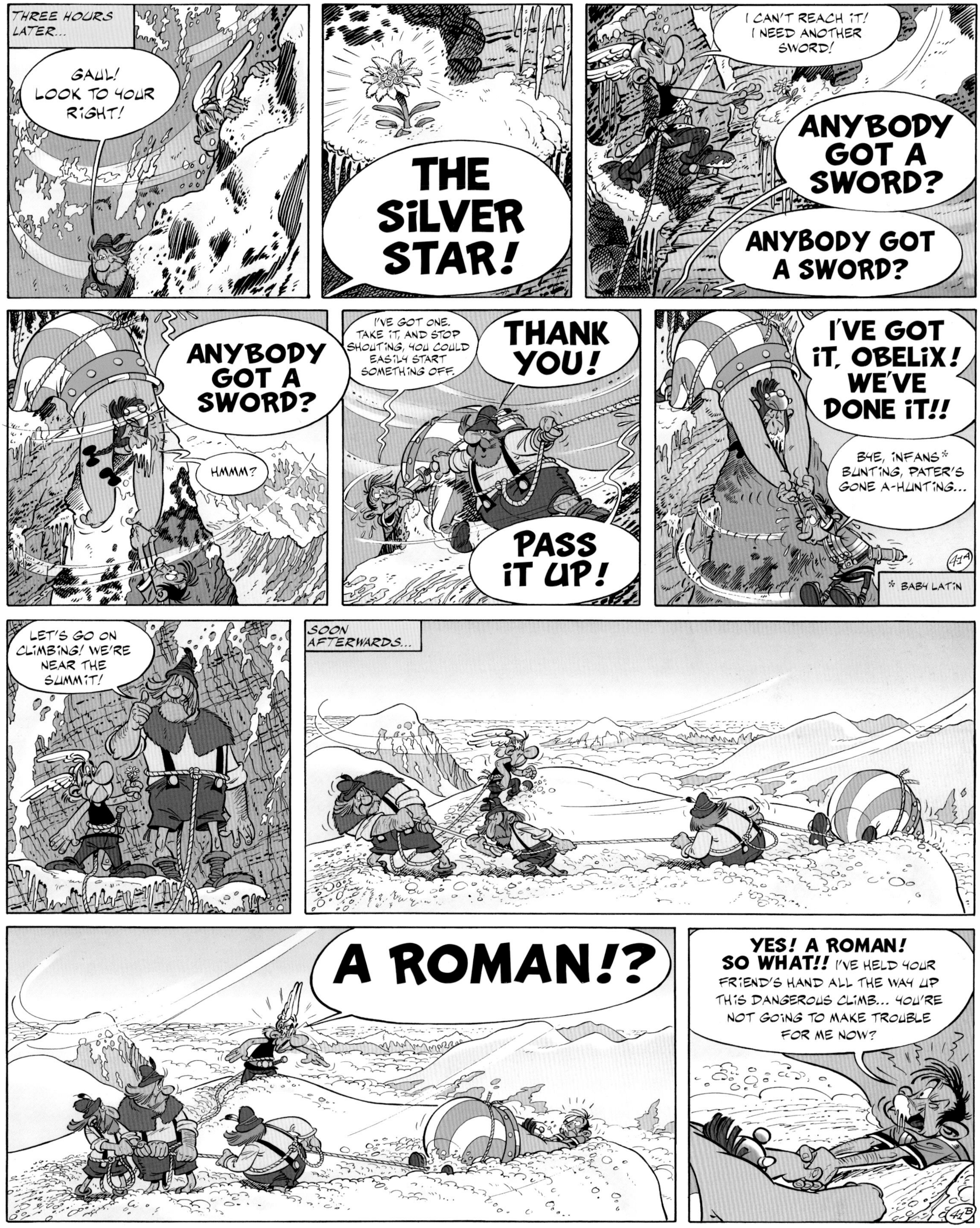
THREE HOURS LATER...
GAUL! LOOK TO YOUR RIGHT!
THE SILVER STAR!
I CAN'T REACH IT! I NEED ANOTHER SWORD!
ANYBODY GOT A SWORD?
ANYBODY GOT A SWORD?
ANYBODY GOT A SWORD?
HMMM?
I'VE GOT ONE. TAKE IT, AND STOP SHOUTING, YOU COULD EASILY START SOMETHING OFF.
THANK YOU!
PASS IT UP!
I'VE GOT IT, OBELIX! WE'VE DONE IT!!
BYE, INFANS* BUNTING, PATER'S GONE A-HUNTING...
* BABY LATIN
LET'S GO ON CLIMBING! WE'RE NEAR THE SUMMIT!
SOON AFTERWARDS...
A ROMAN!?
YES! A ROMAN! SO WHAT!! I'VE HELD YOUR FRIEND'S HAND ALL THE WAY UP THIS DANGEROUS CLIMB... YOU'RE NOT GOING TO MAKE TROUBLE FOR ME NOW?

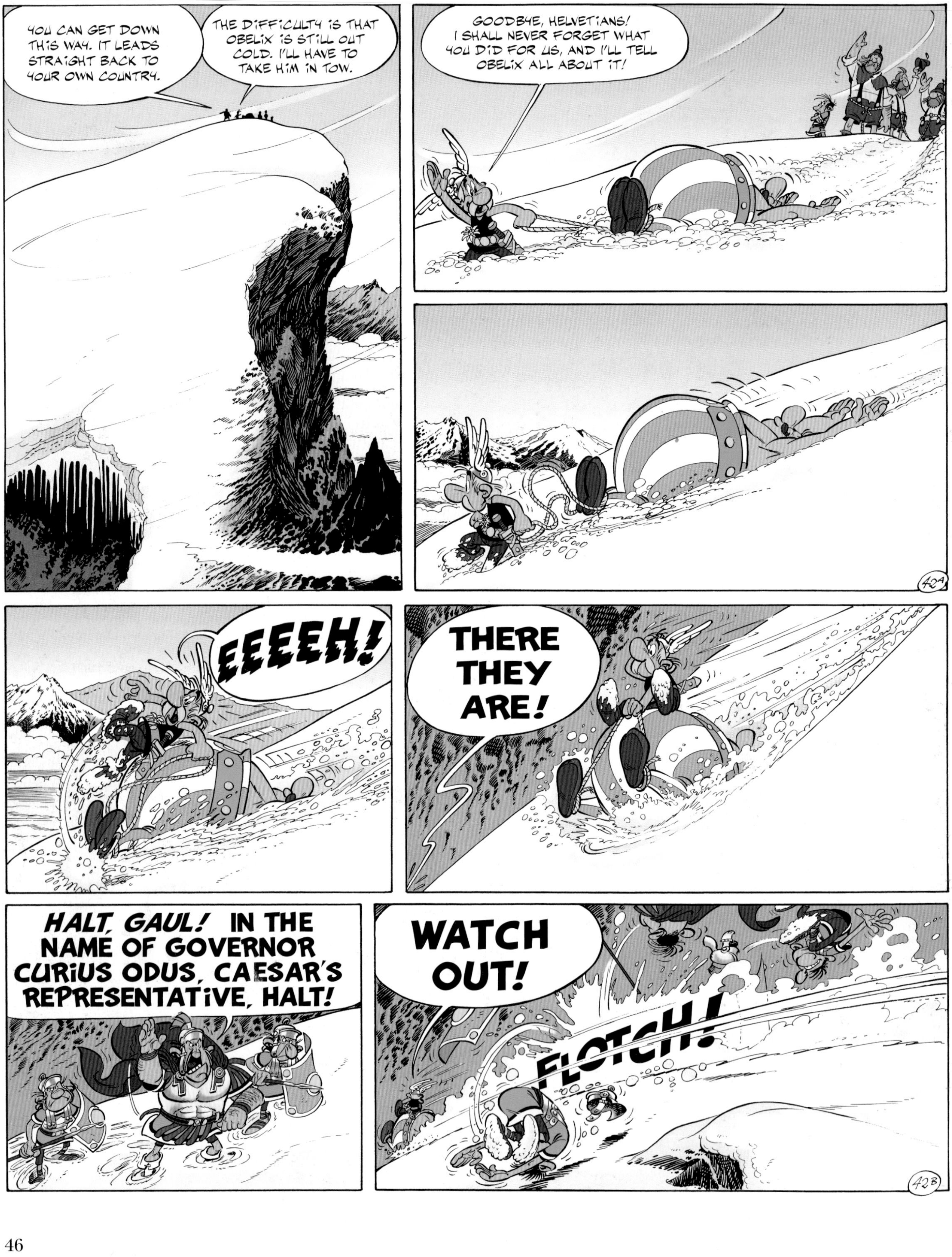

YOU CAN GET DOWN THIS WAY. IT LEADS STRAIGHT BACK TO YOUR OWN COUNTRY.
THE DIFFICULTY IS THAT OBELIX IS STILL OUT COLD. I'LL HAVE TO TAKE HIM IN TOW.
GOODBYE, HELVETIANS! I SHALL NEVER FORGET WHAT YOU DID FOR US, AND I'LL TELL OBELIX ALL ABOUT IT!
42A
EEEEH!
THERE THEY ARE!
HALT, GAUL! IN THE NAME OF GOVERNOR CURIUS ODUS, CAESAR'S REPRESENTATIVE, HALT!
WATCH OUT!
FLOTCH!
42B

45

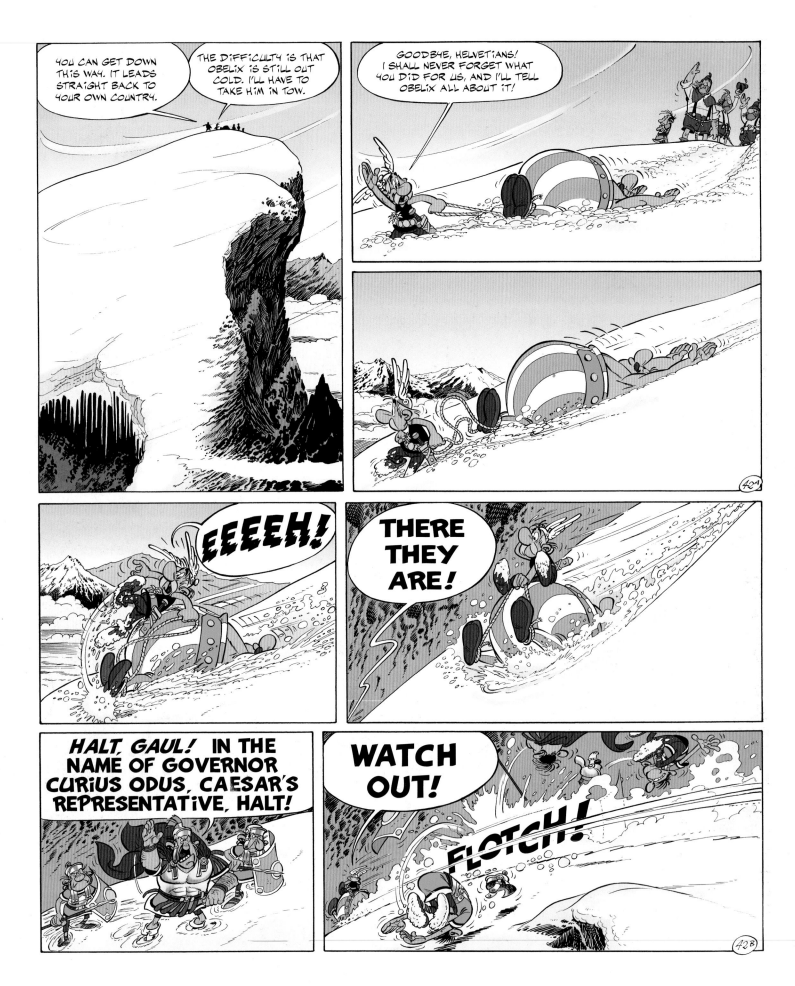

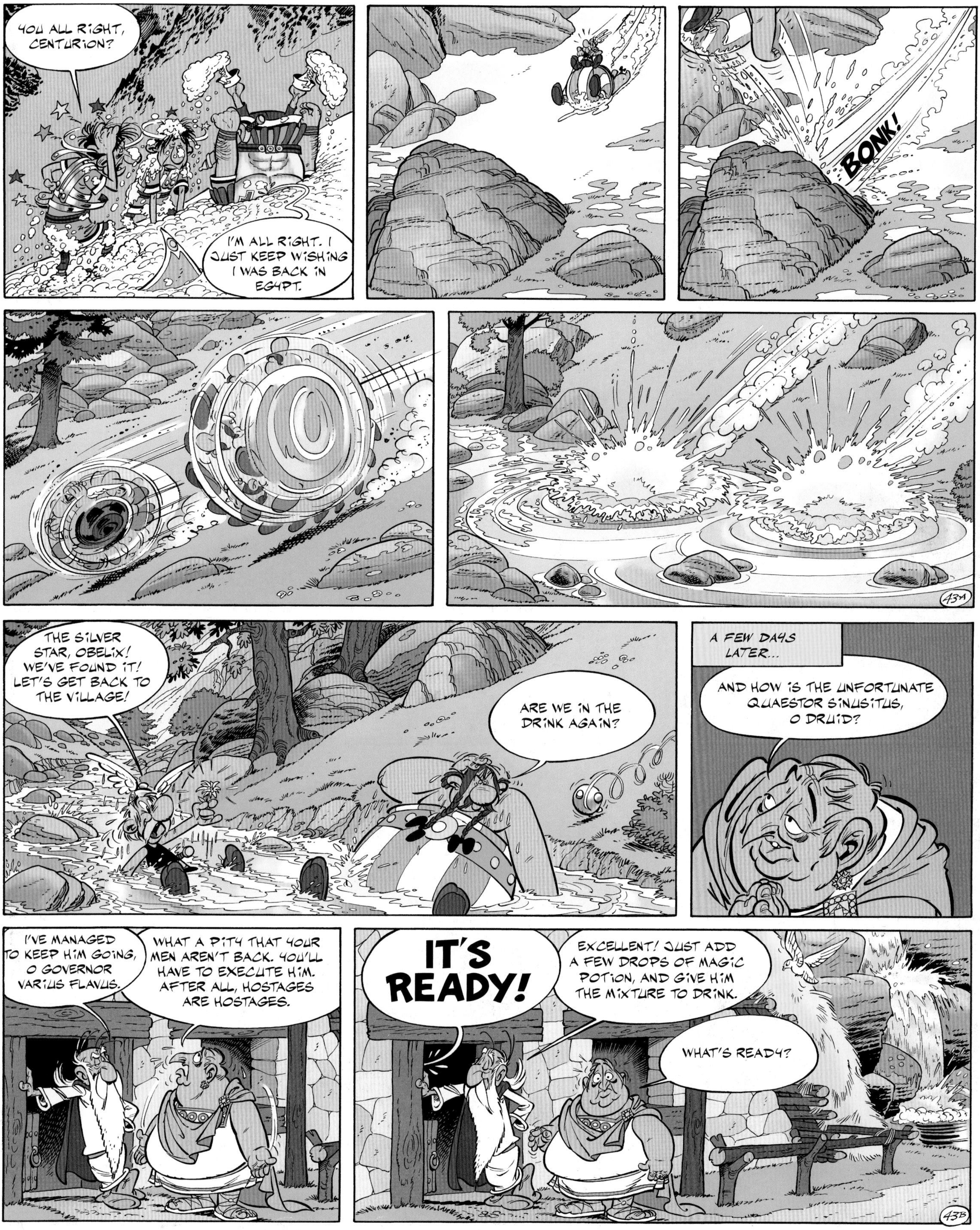
YOU ALL RIGHT, CENTURION?
I'M ALL RIGHT. I JUST KEEP WISHING I WAS BACK IN EGYPT.
BONK!
43A
THE SILVER STAR, OBELIX! WE'VE FOUND IT! LET'S GET BACK TO THE VILLAGE!
ARE WE IN THE DRINK AGAIN?
A FEW DAYS LATER...
AND HOW IS THE UNFORTUNATE QUAESTOR SINUSITUS, O DRUID?
I'VE MANAGED TO KEEP HIM GOING, O GOVERNOR VARIUS FLAVUS.
WHAT A PITY THAT YOUR MEN AREN'T BACK. YOU'LL HAVE TO EXECUTE HIM. AFTER ALL, HOSTAGES ARE HOSTAGES.
IT'S READY!
EXCELLENT! JUST ADD A FEW DROPS OF MAGIC POTION, AND GIVE HIM THE MIXTURE TO DRINK.
WHAT'S READY?
43B

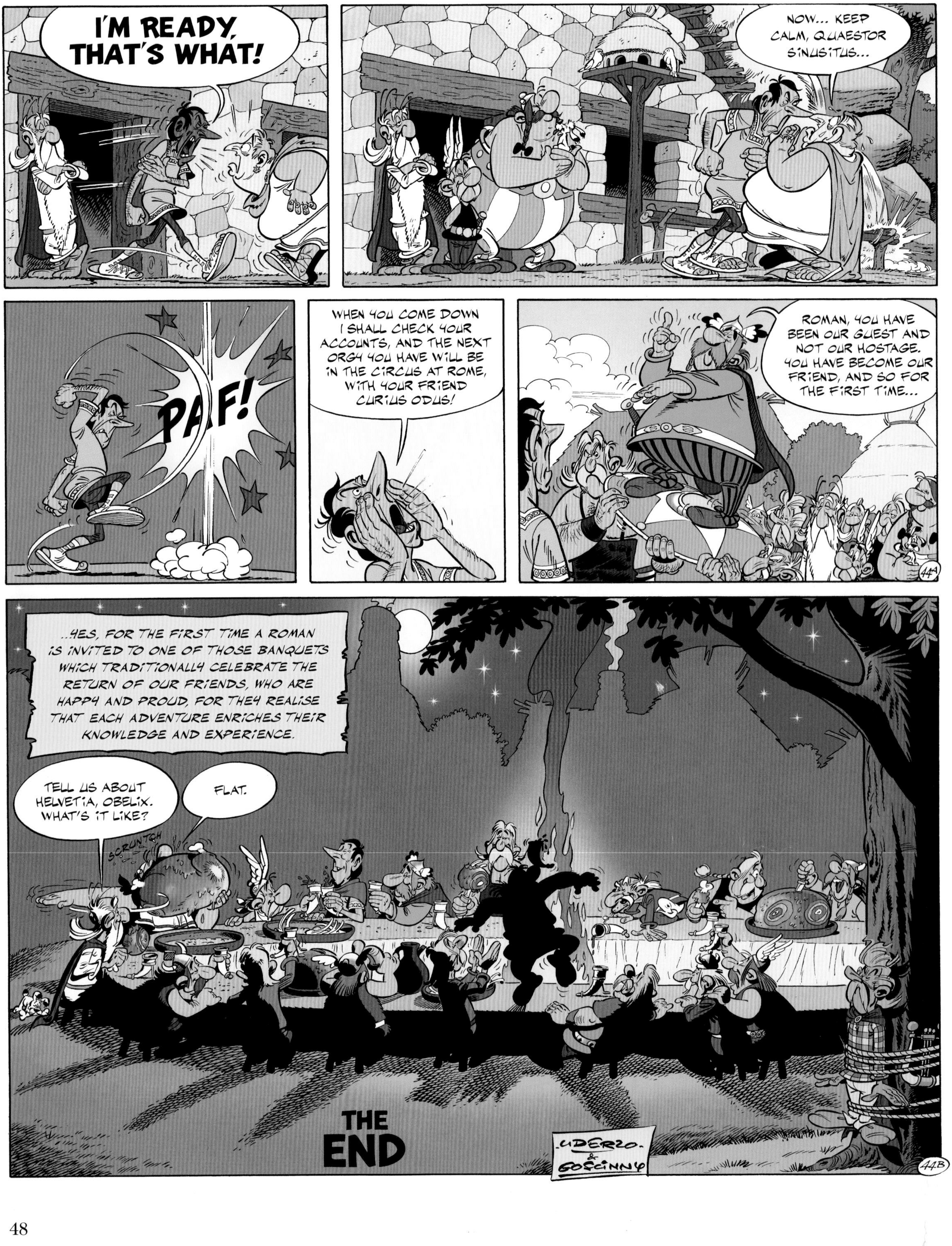
I'M READY, THAT'S WHAT!
NOW... KEEP CALM, QUAESTOR SINUSITUS...
PAF!
WHEN YOU COME DOWN I SHALL CHECK YOUR ACCOUNTS, AND THE NEXT ORGY YOU HAVE WILL BE IN THE CIRCUS AT ROME, WITH YOUR FRIEND CURIUS ODUS!
ROMAN, YOU HAVE BEEN OUR GUEST AND NOT OUR HOSTAGE. YOU HAVE BECOME OUR FRIEND, AND SO FOR THE FIRST TIME...
44A
...YES, FOR THE FIRST TIME A ROMAN IS INVITED TO ONE OF THOSE BANQUETS WHICH TRADITIONALLY CELEBRATE THE RETURN OF OUR FRIENDS, WHO ARE HAPPY AND PROUD, FOR THEY REALISE THAT EACH ADVENTURE ENRICHES THEIR KNOWLEDGE AND EXPERIENCE.
TELL US ABOUT HELVETIA, OBELIX. WHAT'S IT LIKE?
FLAT.
SCRUNTCH
THE END
UDERZO & GOSCINNY
44B

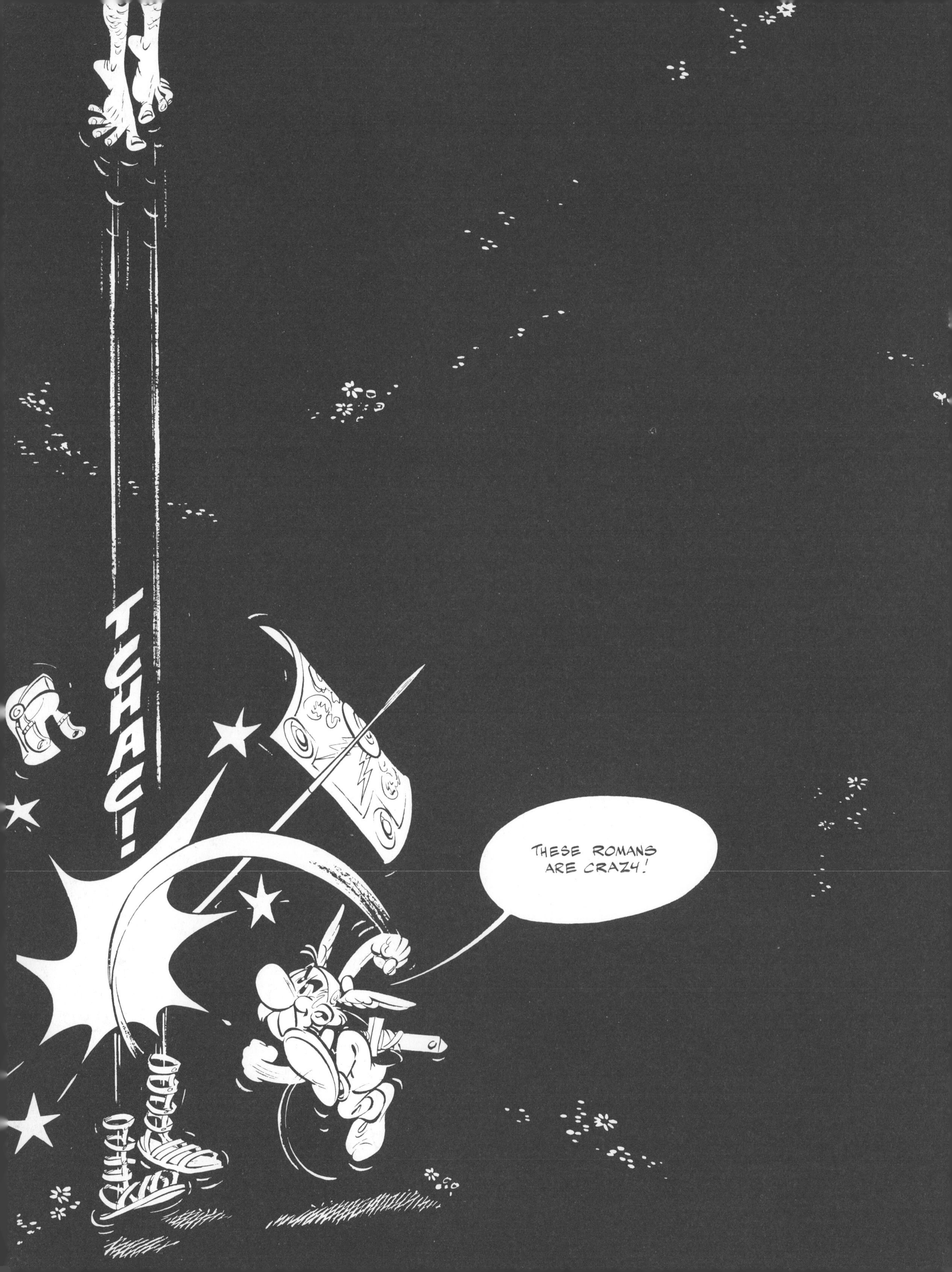
TCHAC!!
THESE ROMANS ARE CRAZY!